THE BROKEN POT

THE BROKEN POT

CAT MIRANDA MYSTERY #3

C.J. SHANE

Published by Rope's End Publishing

ISBN:
print: 978-1-951524-21-0
ebook: 978-1-951524-22-7

Typesetting services by BOOKOW.COM

Acknowledgments

Sincere thanks go to graphic designer Lynne East-Itkin for the lovely book cover and to Dawn Lewis of County Durham, England, for editorial services and for making my English characters speak English English, not American English.

Letty Valdez Mysteries

Desert Jade 2017
Dragon's Revenge 2018
Daemon Waters 2019
Direct Evidence 2022

Cat Miranda Mysteries

Kissed 2020
Fair Play 2021
The Broken Pot 2022

Contents

1 THE BROKEN POT

Brett Jamison slowed his brisk stride along the downtown stretch of Tombstone Canyon Road in Bisbee, Arizona. He took a deep breath and pulled his cell phone from his pocket. He could easily make out the date, Friday, the fifth day of December, and the time, six forty-six in the morning. The sun wouldn't come up until just after seven or so, but his little hometown in southeastern Arizona was already bathed in what was called morning "civil twilight." Already there was enough light for him to see everything and, although shadows persisted, the light was getting stronger by the minute.

He looked up the street and sighed. The purpose of these early morning walks was to get some exercise before Brett went to work in his art studio. An even deeper purpose, though, was to give him a chance to think. There was something about walking, especially in the brisk winter air, which made it easier for him to shut out the clutter in his mind and focus.

Focus on what? On her, of course. Hannah West. Brett fell like an idiot. He'd been struggling with his landlord for over a year to be able to stay in his studio. The bastard landlord had tried his best to renege on Brett's lease – a four-year lease, no less – so he could raise the rent or sell the place. Brett finally won, thanks to a lot of support from the Bisbee artist community and a very good lawyer named Ana Hernandez.

Then, one Saturday in late summer, Hannah had walked in to the studio with a couple of friends to see his work. She left with a small painting and, unbeknownst to her, she left with Brett's heart, too. He never had believed in the idea of love at first sight until he met Hannah. Now he was a total believer, because that was exactly what had happened to him. Theirs was instant attraction that quickly transformed into enchanted love. Hannah started to visit Bisbee frequently, and she always made time to visit Brett's studio. They began to see each other. Then they became lovers.

But Hannah lived in Tucson, and she had only begun her career as an elementary school teacher a few months earlier. As a result, Brett and Hannah saw each other only on weekends, and not even every weekend. Saturdays were his big studio tour and sale days, so he rarely left Bisbee on the weekends. That meant that it was Hannah who usually came to visit, but even so, she wasn't free every weekend. Brett didn't want to move to Tucson. He liked living in Bisbee, and he had that solid four-year lease now. Hannah had just started her new job, and it was too soon for her to resign and begin a new job in the middle of the school year. So they were often apart.

Today was Friday. Hannah would arrive tomorrow by midmorning or maybe a little later. What should he say to her? Be casual, as if he didn't have all these tormented feelings? Tell her he was going home with her to Tucson? Or beg her to stay here in Bisbee with him forever? Or something he hadn't thought of yet?

Leave it to you, you idiot, Brett chided himself. Fall in love with someone who lives nearly one hundred miles away. What a dumbass. He wanted nothing more than to see Hannah every day, to be with her every day, to eat dinner with her every evening, to cuddle with her all night every night. He began walking again, this time at a slower pace, hoping to ease his confused and aching heart.

Brett heard footsteps behind him, so he stepped off the sidewalk into the recessed doorway of one of the street's shops. Above the shop was a hotel for tourists with a wide balcony that extended out toward the street above the shop's entrance. A staircase a couple of doors down led to the hotel's entrance on the second floor. Brett turned to see who was behind him.

Renata Romero, the manager of Bisbee's most popular bar, the Star Tavern, was jogging up Tombstone Canyon Road. She was dressed in athletic pants and a sweatshirt, and she was making progress at moderate pace on the other side of the street. As she came closer, she saw Brett, and they exchanged smiles and waves.

Before Renata could take another step, there was a sudden, loud crash in the middle of the street. Renata stopped, and both she and Brett stared at what appeared to be a large piece of pottery that had broken on impact into shards of many sizes and shapes. Before either of them could move, another, much larger object, came hurtling over the upper balcony's railing. This time it was a human body, a woman's body. The woman crashed onto the pavement, landing in a crumpled heap not far from the broken pot. There was no movement or sound coming from her still body.

Brett stood there, aghast. He looked up at Renata, but she wasn't looking at him or at the dead woman in the street. She was staring up at something, or someone, on the hotel balcony above Brett. Suddenly, Renata turned back toward the direction she'd come from, but this time, she was running – a full out sprint as fast as she could go. Brett followed her with his eyes.

Within seconds, a man rapidly descended the hotel stairs to street level. By the time he reached the street, he was in a full run with all his attention directed toward Renata. He never noticed Brett. He was focused entirely on Renata, pursuing her at top speed. After only a moment, the man slowed and paused, peering along the street to the east, then to the west and south.

Brett watched the man intently. The stranger was dressed in an ivory-colored suit in a trendy, fashionable style. He was wearing highly polished loafers and his dark hair was styled in a longish cut that just reached his shoulder. He looked like a man with money. Brett had never seen him before. It was obvious to Brett that the man was chasing Renata. But, by this time, she was nowhere to be seen. It looked to Brett that Renata had outrun the man, and she'd managed to disappear before he could catch her. The man turned and headed back toward Brett and to the hotel stairs he'd just descended moments before.

When Brett saw the man returning, he stepped back into the shop door recess where the man couldn't see him. He could hear the man coming toward him, and he heard the man pause at the foot of the stairs. Brett guessed he was looking at the woman's body on the street. Lucky for Brett, he did not approach the body. Instead, he climbed back up the stairs to the hotel on the second story.

Brett held very still. He heard a door open and close. Then there was nothing but quiet. He couldn't hear any sounds at all on the balcony above him from where the woman's body had fallen. Or maybe she'd been thrown. He couldn't say for sure. Brett's rational mind began to return after the shock of seeing the body in the street and what seemed to be a threat to Renata from the fashionably-dressed stranger. Brett stepped toward the woman, but before he even knelt for a closer look, he could tell she was dead. She was white as a sheet, her lips were a faint blue color, and her neck was at an impossible angle, obviously broken. He reached out and touched her neck. No pulse. She was cold, too.

Brett returned to the shadowed recess and pulled his cell phone from his pocket to make two quick calls. First, he called for an ambulance, and next, he called the local police department. He looked around. Streaks of early morning sunlight were visible now on the tops of the Mule Mountains that rose above Bisbee's downtown streets. Full daylight would soon be upon the entire town.

The wail of an ambulance siren floated toward Brett. There were still no sounds above him. He stepped back into the street and used his cell phone to take a photo of the woman and a second photo of the broken pot. Later, he wouldn't be able to say for sure why he took these photos. It was just a sudden impulse. He returned to the recess in the shadows, and he waited. The flashing lights of both an ambulance and police car were coming toward him. He decided that, after he talked to the police, he'd go look for Renata and make sure she was okay.

~~~

Cat Miranda stood at the back wall of her art gallery, arms folded across her chest. She smiled. The gallery looked good, and Cat was satisfied with the new exhibit. It was Friday afternoon and she already had most of the paintings hung for the art opening tomorrow on Saturday evening. She'd left space for Brett Jamison's work and a couple of other artists, too, all of whom tended to be slow in bringing in new artwork. Cat was so glad to be able to represent Brett. Two of his abstract landscapes had sold a couple of weeks earlier to an enthusiastic, art-loving couple from Minneapolis who had come to visit Bisbee in the winter. Cat had this feeling that Brett was an up-and-coming artist, and she would do what she could to help him become successful. And she liked him. Brett was a nice guy.

Just then, Cat heard a soft knock on the gallery door. She looked up and saw Brett peering in through the large glass window. She hurried to open the door.

"Speak of the devil," Cat said. "I was just thinking about you. Come on in." She noticed immediately that Brett, who was usually cheerful, had a serious, even worried, look on his face.

"Hi, Cat." Brett brushed a strand of brown hair away from his eyes. "I need to get a haircut," he muttered to himself. He looked at Cat who was smiling at him. "I can't seem to find enough time to do everything that needs to be done."

"That's okay. Don't worry. One step at a time. What did you bring me?"

Brett looked down at the large leather case in his hand. "I have a couple of works, both oils and not too large. Both are twenty by twenty-four inches."
~~~

"That's a good size, very popular among the tourists. Not so difficult to carry or ship home, but big enough to look good on the living room wall."

Brett pulled the two works from the case. One painting was easy to identify as Bisbee and the surrounding Mule Mountains. It was painted with strong brushstrokes of blues and greens. The second painting featured streaks of red and orange in the sky reflected on a distant desert mountain.

"Oh, nice!" Cat said. "You're getting to be well known for your intense colors."

"These are obviously landscapes, even if fairly abstract. But sometimes I get this urge to go abstract all the way. I always admired the Color Field painters, especially Frankenthaler."

"Me too. Mark Rothko is my favorite. So this blue-green one looks like Old Bisbee after a rain."

"That's what I call it. 'After the Rain.'"

"And this one?"

"I call it 'Sunset.' Not very original, I know. I never have been any good at titles."

Cat shook her head. "I think people will be looking more at the painting than at the title. Your titles are just fine. Stop worrying."

Brett shook his head. "Sorry, Cat. Today isn't such a great day for me. Something bad happened this morning, and it put me sort of in a negative state of mind."

Cat's eyebrows went up. "What's going on? Want to tell me?"

"Did you hear about the woman who died on the street downtown early this morning?"

"*No!* Who died? What happened?"

"I don't know who she was. I had stopped for a few minutes on my morning walk. I saw Renata Romero jogging up street. All of a sudden, someone threw a big ceramic pot off the balcony from above my head into the street. A couple of seconds later, this woman came flying off. She crashed onto the pavement just like the pot. Maybe she threw the pot and then jumped. I don't know. But she was like…so dead."

"Good grief. That's terrible. Where was this?"

"East-West Hotel. You know, on Tombstone Canyon Road."

"Does Sam Morales know about this?"

"Yes, I called the police first thing. And I called an ambulance, too, but it was too late for her. She was beyond help."

"A suicide? Or some kind of accident? No idea?" Cat could see the distress on Brett's face. He had a reputation as being an upbeat, friendly fellow. But now, the frown on his face was fixed.

"No. I'm clueless. This was bad enough, but things got even weirder. Before the woman hit the pavement, I saw Renata Romero out jogging." He paused. "I said that already, didn't I?" He sighed.

"You're doing fine, Brett." Cat reached out and patted him on his shoulder.

"Okay. So Renata was across the street from me. When the pot and the woman crashed into the street, I saw Renata looking up above me at something. Then she took off running really fast back toward where she'd come from, down the street toward the center of town. A second later, this guy came running down the steps after her. I'm guessing he was the one that Renata was looking at. I saw him run after her. Then he came back about only a few minutes later."

"Do you think he had anything to do with the woman coming off the balcony?"

"I don't know. The woman might have jumped. Or maybe he pushed her. And I don't know why the guy tried to follow Renata, but I don't think he found her. I saw him looking but I guess he couldn't see her so he came back. But by then, I checked on the woman. Definitely dead. Then I called the cops. Sam Morales, I mean. He's the only cop I know."

"I'm surprised Sam is still here. I heard he was going to take a vacation with his family. He hired a new deputy recently to take some of the load from him because he works so many hours. I haven't met the new deputy yet. So what did Sam say?"

"Not much. He asked me a bunch of questions, and I told him everything I knew, which wasn't much really. I told him what I just told you. Then the ambulance came and took away the woman's body. After that, Sam told me I could go."

"And the pot?"

Brett shrugged his shoulders. "I don't know. I was kind of shaken up. After I talked to Sam, I went down the street to see if I could find Renata. I know she lives above the Star Tavern, and I could see lights on in her apartment. I figured she was okay. I didn't want to bother her so I went back to my studio. About that pot, the pieces may still be there in the street. Or not. I don't know what happened to the pot."

"That's weird. I'm sorry that happened. I understand why you might be disturbed."

"Yeah, well, tomorrow my girlfriend is coming, and she always makes me feel good. So I have that to look forward to."

"My *novio* is coming tomorrow, too. So we both have something to look forward to. You and your girlfriend are coming to the opening tomorrow?"

"Yes, Hannah and I will see you then. As for me, I'm going back to my studio now and try to chill the rest of the day." He headed toward the front door. At the last minute, Brett turned to Cat and said, "Thanks, Cat."

"No problem. See you tomorrow, Brett." Cat closed the door to the gallery behind Brett and locked it. She turned back to begin the task of hanging Brett's two new paintings.

2 ARRIVALS

Cat stretched and yawned. She sat up in bed and looked over at the two dogs lying on their pillows not far from the foot of her bed. They were both staring at her, eyes bright. Tito began wagging his tail. Cat felt a sudden wave of emotion wash over her. She loved these dogs.

First was her beloved Tito, the very big, black Great Dane that she had rescued from Bisbee's animal shelter. Cat loved him with all her heart. After all, Tito had rescued her from a criminal who threatened to shoot her. Next to Tito was his daughter, Greta, black-and-white puppy Greta, full-of-energy Greta, seven months old Greta, jump-up-and-down Greta, Greta the puppy who was wearing everyone out — even Tito. Cat hoped that when Miles returned, he would take Greta for a long run and release some of that puppy energy for a few hours. Cat loved Greta, too, even though she was a lot of trouble. Greta wasn't really Cat's dog. She belonged to Ian Trevelyan, Miles's dad, and his new wife, Amanda Fontaine, now Amanda Trevelyan. Cat was taking care of Greta while Ian and Amanda were traveling in Great Britain and on the European continent.

"Okay, you two. You're going outside first. You can pee on everything and, by the time you finish, I'll have your breakfast ready. Then we'll go for a walk. Before that, though, I'm making myself some coffee." Now Greta's tail was wagging, too.

Cat fulfilled her promise. Breakfast for the dogs, coffee for Cat, then breakfast for Cat. Finally, the three of them took their long morning walk on the hillside trail above Bisbee. As usual, Tito was polite on their walk. Greta, not so much. She constantly pulled on the leash even though Cat repeatedly reminded her not to pull. Greta wagged her tail, didn't pull for a couple of minutes, then began pulling again. After about half an hour, Cat gave up. They headed home again.

"Okay. I'm going over to the gallery now," she said to the dogs after tidying up the kitchen. "I have some new paintings to hang before tonight's opening. It's sunny in the back yard so that's where you two are going. Here's your ball." She led them into the fenced backyard and threw out a ball. Greta went after it. Greta snatched the ball up in her mouth, looked at Cat, tail wagging, and then dropped the ball. The idea of bringing it back had not yet occurred to Greta. Tito watched, tail wagging.

"Try to be good," Cat said, as she closed the backdoor.

Ten minutes later, Cat was standing in the middle of her high-ceilinged art gallery. She looked around for the right place to put four additional paintings, all ready to hang. One was a large desert landscape, more realistic than many of the paintings in the exhibit. Over there, she thought, as she stared at a space on the eastern wall. The second painting was smaller, a portrait of a Bisbee street musician. She found a place for it next to another painting of similar size. She turned and held up one of Brett Jamison's abstract landscapes, the one titled "After the Rain." Over there, closer to the front door, she muttered to herself. His painting would be visible from the street through the big front windows when the gallery was closed. That is, if it didn't sell tonight. Brett's paintings sold well. The other painting, "Sunset," found its home, too. This was the final painting to go up, and Cat now considered the exhibit ready for potential collectors.

With all four paintings now up on the wall, along with quite a few more, she stood back and turned around in a circle, looking at everything. Good, good, good, she thought to herself. She just wished her brother Luis was still alive to see how the gallery was doing. He would have been so proud of everything, and proud of his little sister, too. Cat felt that familiar sadness in her chest. Luis was too young to die, taken by that awful illness. Oh, she missed her big brother.

Cat stopped for a moment to reflect on the conversation that she'd had the day before with Brett Jamison when he came in with his artwork. She didn't know what to make of a dead person on Tombstone Canyon Road. Maybe tomorrow she could look into this and find out more about what had happened.

Okay, Cat said to herself. Let's set aside these dark thoughts and move on. What's next on the agenda? Eat lunch, take a little siesta, then come back to the gallery and wait upstairs for Miles Trevelyan who would be arriving soon. Miles, her *novio*, her deeply-loved sweetheart.

***

Later that afternoon, Cat sat in a comfy chair on the upstairs open-air deck of her art gallery. Behind her was the sliding glass door that led into her office where she met with her graphics design clients. Downstairs, the gallery took up most of the first floor. There was also a storage room and a small kitchen at the rear of the gallery that led outside to the back. Cat was reading a book as she sat on the deck. Or, she was trying to read a book. In reality, she was waiting impatiently for Miles Trevelyan to show up. He was driving into Bisbee from Tucson on this early December afternoon, and Cat couldn't wait to see him. He'd left her, as usual, early on Monday morning and drove to Tucson where he taught at the University of Arizona during the week. But instead of returning to Bisbee on Friday afternoon as he'd always done throughout the autumn, this time he'd waited until the next day, Saturday, to return. He had agreed to pick up two visitors from the Tucson airport, a couple of Brits, Trevor Davies and Trevor's sister Fiona. Miles had met Trevor on his last trip to England and, when Trevor and his sister expressed an interest in seeing Bisbee, Miles agreed to help by giving them a ride.

Cat looked down at the two dogs lounging on huge pillows on the deck near her. Earlier, she decided to bring them up to the deck with her to wait for Miles. Cat looked back at the book, then at Tombstone Canyon Road, then at the dogs, then back to the book. She sighed. It was taking Miles forever to arrive. Cat was madly in love with Miles, and he with her. Their weekday separations were difficult for both, but the reunions every long weekend were intensely happy.

Finally! She could see Miles turning from Tombstone Canyon Road onto her street, driving up toward the art gallery, and pulling into gallery's driveway. By the time he'd parked his car, Cat, Tito, and Greta had all gone downstairs and all exploded from the back door of the gallery. Cat ran to Miles, threw her arms around him and kissed him repeatedly. Miles was laughing as he returned her kisses. The dogs bounced around, wagging their tails and bumping happily into Miles, intent on welcoming him home.

"I'm glad to see you, too." Miles reached out and petted the two canine heads. He then turned and gestured to the two passengers who were climbing out of his car. "I have two fellow Brits for you to meet."

"Hi. *Hola*," Cat said with a big grin on her face. "Welcome to Bisbee."

Trevor Davies came forward and shook Cat's hand. "Thank you for the warm welcome. I think Miles probably told you. I'm an ornithologist. That is, I'm a total bird nerd. I hope to do some serious birdwatching while I'm here. Miles tells me this is a great place to see several species."

"More than five hundred species in our state," Cat said. "We're in the Pacific Flyway."

By that time, the other passenger, a young woman, had come around the car to greet everyone, but she saw the dogs first. She dropped immediately to her knees. Greta came close and began licking her face. The young woman put her arms around Greta who was trembling with excitement, her tail wagging vigorously.

"Oh, look at you! You are so beautiful." Greta licked her face again.

"Hi," Cat said. "I'm Cat Miranda. Welcome to Bisbee. I see you like dogs."

"Hello. I'm Fiona Davies, Trevor's sister." She kissed Greta's muzzle. "I love dogs, especially big dogs." She stood and exchanged handshakes with Cat. "What's this beauty's name? And how about this big boy? What's his name?" She reached down to stroke Tito's head.

"This is Tito. He's a very good boy. And that's Greta. She's still a puppy and a bit on the rowdy side. Are you a birder, too?"

Fiona shrugged. "I like birds, and I have a couple of bird feeders at home. But I'm not a birder like my brother. Really, I'm a journalist, mainly freelance writing for magazines. I'm hoping to get some good stories to write about while I'm in southern Arizona. I'm always investigating topics for articles like nice places to visit, good food options, fun things to do," Fiona turned and smiled at her brother, "and so I'll be on the lookout for story ideas. I'm just here for a short time. I've been in this part of the world for several months already. I spent a little time in Mexico City, and I've already visited several places in the American Southwest. Taos Pueblo, the Grand Canyon, Four Corners, places like that. Southern California, too. Several of my articles have been published already. When I got an email from my brother about his visit here, I decided to join him for a bit. I'll be heading back to England soon."

"Are you traveling around, too, Trevor?" Cat asked.

Trevor made a face that turned into a grin. "Who knows? My job as a conservationist was defunded. In fact, the conservation group I was working for doesn't exist anymore because it merged with a larger, older organization. They told me they were applying for a grant to hire me in a new position, but that could take a while. Or I might decide to work for some other organization. Really, I don't know. I don't really have a definite plan right now.

I thought I needed a change for a while so I decided to take a holiday. I heard about Miles's dad and his birding tours so I thought I'd check it out. I doubt I'll be wandering around as much as Fiona because I'm into natural areas, and it looks like there are a lot of great things to see here. Those saguaros we saw in the Tucson area are magnificent."

"I assume you two will be staying with us tonight?" Cat smiled.

"Really?" Trevor said. "I thought we'd have to rent a motel room."

"Nah. I have plenty of room. See that house next door to the gallery? Miles and I share a bedroom. There's a guest bedroom for one of you, and the other can sleep either in Miles's library or in my little art studio. We have an inflatable mattress. You and Fiona can decide who goes where."

"I'll be a gentleman and let my big sister have the guest bedroom," Trevor said.

Fiona grinned and punched him on his arm. "You're trying to make up for torturing me when we were kids." She turned to Cat. "It's very kind of you to host us," she said.

"Fiona, I hope you are interested in art as a topic to write about. Bisbee is a real arts destination. There are several galleries here, not just mine. And I'm hosting an opening tonight at my gallery. I hope you'll come. I can introduce you to everyone."

"I'd be delighted," Fiona said. "Trevor?"

"Absolutely. Sounds like fun."

"Okay. So I suggest you unload your luggage, and we'll get you set up in my house."

"Then eat? It's past time for tea." Miles asked.

"Tea?" Cat chuckled. "Maybe supper, you mean? You three go down to Jillie's and get a meal there. You can explain all about the Sonoran specialties to Fiona and Trevor."

"Yeah," Miles said with a grin. "Jillie makes nopalito jam. It's made of nopal pads. Nopal is a cactus."

Trevor grinned. "Count me in."

Fiona had a rather unsure look on her face. "Well, I'll try it. That sounds a bit weird, but I like to try new foods. Maybe I can put eating a cactus into one of my articles."

"I'll get a snack," Cat said. "It's time for me to start setting things up for the opening. After you finish eating, you can come back and help me. So scoot on out of here."

Miles kissed her. He turned to Trevor and Fiona. "We can walk. It's not far from here."

"Before you go, Miles, let's find a little time alone later. I have a story to tell you about a woman who died here recently. Maybe she was murdered."

His eyebrows went up. "That's not good. Yes, I want to hear all about it."

Fiona, Trevor, and Miles carried luggage into Cat's house. Then the three Brits set off walking toward Jillie's restaurant.

Cat fed Tito and Greta their supper, then she turned on the television. Earlier, Cat had discovered that every time she left the dogs alone, Greta stayed a little calmer if she could hear human voices making human sounds. Television talk shows turned out to be the best for that. The voices seemed to reassure Greta's puppy mind that all was well. Cat ate her snack, and then she headed back to the art gallery.

3 THE OPENING

Almost two hours later, Cat looked around the gallery and smiled with pleasure at seeing the crowd that had gathered to attend her latest gallery art opening. The Saturday night openings at her gallery had become something of a community social event, with both locals and tourists attending. Most of the visitors had a cup of wine in hand, and they were all either chatting with each other or slowly making their way around the room and looking at the art. She liked the hum of conversation that she could hear coming from all corners. She'd already made several sales, too.

This opening was special because, for the first time, Cat had hired a musician to play for her guests. She looked over at a young man sitting in a chair, a violin on his shoulder with one hand on the strings and the other holding a bow. Luca Sutherland. That was his name. He was fairly new to Bisbee, and Cat didn't know him well at all. But she loved his music, and she was very glad that he was here. She definitely would invite him back to play for more openings.

"Hey, Cat. This has to be one of your best events." A casually-dressed man, his brown hair pulled back into a long braid, approached her. He was holding a cup of red wine.

Cat Miranda turned toward Michael Dimaio and grinned. "Thanks, Michael. There's a good crowd here tonight."

Willow Dimaio appeared at her husband's side. All three turned to survey the large main room of the gallery with its polished wooden floor and high ceiling.

Cat turned back to Michael and Willow. "Do you have any news about the theft at your pottery shop?"

"No." Michael shook his head and frowned. "Whoever took that pot just walked out with it. Too bad. We had to pay the dealer in advance for it, and the idea was to mark it up some so we'd make a little profit. We lost money when it was stolen. Now we get nothing."

"We're going to check the neighbor's shop to see if their security video was on," Willow added. "We hope to get a view of the person who stole the pot."

"What do you know about the pot's origin?" Cat was curious about pottery. Actually, she was curious about anything having to do with arts and fine crafts.

"It's contemporary, made by a member of the Jemez tribe in northern New Mexico," Michael said. "We bought it and several other pots from a dealer based in Albuquerque. We acquired pots from several different Native American tribes because we wanted to have a good selection for our little mini-gallery."

"I especially liked the colors on the stolen pot, all reds and oranges. Very desert-like," Willow said. "We reported the theft, but there's not much to go on."

"Do you have a photo of the pot?" Cat asked.

"Yes." Michael pulled his cell phone from his pocket, found the photo and handed the phone to Cat.

"Beautiful," she said. "Okay. Now that I know what it looks like, I'll keep an eye out for it."

Michael frowned. "We thought we were being so clever to have a small gallery attached to our pottery shop. Maybe it was a bad idea."

"Don't be discouraged, sweetheart," Willow said. "We're doing something new, and we just have to learn how to do it."

"The police don't have any leads?" Cat asked.

"No. No one saw the theft take place," Michael answered. "That's why we want to see if the thief was caught on video."

"I'm sorry to hear about this," Cat said. "But, Michael, the possibility of theft is always going to be a problem. All the gallery owners in town have to take that into consideration. Me included. Maybe you could consider only opening your gallery a couple of days a week until you can figure out how to keep an eye on everything."

Willow agreed. "Yes, we can keep the pottery shop open every day and the gallery open only when one of us has time to be there. When we're firing pottery in the kiln or waiting for pieces to cool off would work. And, really, Michael, we've had our share of cups and bowls taken from the pottery shop."

Michael nodded. "Okay. I get the message. I shouldn't expect everything to be perfect from day one. I guess we'll figure it out."

"Yes. Just consider your gallery to be a work in progress," Cat said. "Kind of like this gallery. I'd like to see you be successful. By the way, have you heard about the woman who died yesterday on Tombstone Canyon Road?"

"Yes, we heard about that," Willow said. "It's sad and kind of scary. No one knows who she is."

"Did you hear about the broken pot, too? Does that have anything to do with your stolen pot?"

Michael frowned. "No, this is the first I've heard about a broken pot. What do you know about that?"

"Not much really. Brett Jamison said someone threw a big pot out onto the street and a few seconds later, a woman was thrown or jumped. That's not clear. What is clear is that she crashed head-first onto the pavement and died. That's all I know," Cat said.

All three fell silent for a few minutes.

"Okay. Let's forget about this dark stuff for a while." Michael smiled. "I think I'll leave you two for a while and go hand out my card to those folks over there. Maybe they'll want to come by our pottery shop and take home some goodies. Yep, handcrafted coffee mugs direct from the art capital of the world, Bisbee, Arizona. That's what they need." He grinned as he pulled some cards from his shirt pocket and walked toward a small group of guests.

"Hey, look," Willow said. "There's Brett Jamison and his girl-friend."

"Yes, I saw them come in a few minutes ago. One of the locals grabbed him right away. Now it looks like he's talking to a potential collector who asked me earlier about his artwork. Maybe actually meeting Brett will encourage him to buy Brett's painting."

They both watched the crowd for a few minutes.

"Cat, that silk shirt you are wearing is stunning. I love the bright red color."

"Thanks, Willow. I hope the red shirt, black leggings and my boots will make me look like a serious art gallerist and also make me look a little taller."

Willow chuckled. "Oh, it's always something, isn't it? You want to be taller, and I would like to be a little thinner. I'd like to be a willowy Willow."

"You're too voluptuous to be willowy. I love that word 'voluptuous.' That's what Miles calls me. And I thought all this time that I just had big boobs. That's your problem, too. It's hard to be willowy if you are voluptuous."

Willow laughed. "Say, Cat, how is your oh-so articulate, oh-so good-looking boyfriend doing?" She looked over at Miles Trevelyan.

Cat grinned. "Miles is the best thing that's ever happened to me. I'm so lucky. I thought when he left here last winter that I'd never see him again. But we stayed in touch, he came back for a visit, and I went with him when he returned to England for a few months. We went over to the Continent, too, before we returned home. We had a lot of fun. He's working now at that job teaching at the university in Tucson so we see each other frequently. He usually spends Friday afternoon through Monday with me in Bisbee. Then Monday afternoon he goes to Tucson to teach. He comes back home to Bisbee on Fridays. He's still renting a car but he's planning on buying his own. He has an international driver's license."

"Good. I hope sometime you'll tell us all about your trip to Europe with him. I'd love to go to Europe. Maybe someday we'll save up enough money to do that. Who's that guy Miles is talking to? He's cute, too."

"That's Trevor Davies. He's visiting here now. He was working for an ornithology group in southern England so that means he's big into birding. I think he'll stay to see the migrating winter birds. That's his sister over there. Her name is Fiona."

"So they are from England, too?"

Cat laughed. "Yeah, we're being invaded. First Miles. Next his dad, Ian Trevelyan. Now Trevor and Fiona. I doubt Fiona will be here for long though. She's a freelance writer, and she travels around looking for stories to write. She's been in Mexico and the American Southwest for several months. She's going home soon."

Both women turned to look at Fiona Davies who was watching Luca Sutherland play the violin. She was a bit taller than Cat, slender, with shoulder-length brown hair and a very fair complexion.

"Wow. She really looks a lot like her brother," Willow said. "She's very pretty. And she's got her eye on Luca."

"Well, why not? He's a looker, too." They both chuckled. "I met Luca through Mari Spencer," Cat explained. "He does light carpentry work and whatever else she needs to run her business. She's used to working alone, but she's busy enough these days so she hires him part-time. He does music gigs like this around town, too. He's a really wonderful musician."

Both women shifted their attention back to Miles and Trevor. Miles Trevelyan, late twenties, six feet tall, tousled blonde hair, blue eyes, well-built, and handsome beyond belief, according to Cat, was gesturing dramatically. Trevor Davies, the same height as Miles, handsome and well-built, too, shook his head vehemently. He, too, was gesturing. Their voices were becoming louder.

"I'm going to go see what's going on. It sounds like they're arguing," Cat said.

"Guess I'll go find Michael. See you later." Willow waved good-bye.

Cat approached the two Englishmen only to discover that art was far from their minds.

"What are you dudes talking about?"

"Football," Trevor answered. "Miles is crazy. He thinks Manchester United is still the best."

"United is definitely the best," Miles said. "Everyone knows that."

"I say Liverpool is coming on strong and will be the next champions. Or maybe Tottenham Spurs."

"What about Arsenal? You left them out. And you have to use the American term here. Soccer, not football." Miles stuck his chin out.

"Whatever," Trevor answered. His chin was already out there as far as Cat was concerned. Time for her to interrupt.

"You boys behave yourselves. This is my art gallery opening. No fighting about soccer…or football…whatever you want to call it. Try to keep it down." Cat knew these two liked each other and got along well. But this wasn't the time or place to be having a heated conversation about sports. "Or, if you are going to argue about something, you can argue about which painting is the best and who will be the lucky one to buy it and take it home."

"Sorry, Cat. We'll lower our voices," Miles said.

"Yes, sorry. We can talk about football…I mean soccer…another time," Trevor added.

Cat nodded approvingly. "Hey, I have an idea. How about if you two take a little walk to the Star Tavern, drink a beer or ale or whatever together, and continue your conversation there."

Both men turned to Cat, grins on their faces. "Good idea," they both said at once.

"Get going and save some red wine for me."

"I'm for a pint of stout, but I don't want to leave you. I don't like the idea of you walking downtown on your own." Miles tended to be protective of Cat after he had rescued her from a killer.

"If you insist. Please ask Fiona if she wants to go, too. And you two try to keep it down."

Miles leaned down and kissed Cat. "I will *quietly* convince Trevor that he doesn't know what the hell he's talking about."

Trevor laughed. He whispered dramatically, "No way. Liverpool rules."

"I'm going to ignore that," Miles chuckled.

The two men approached Fiona.

"Want to come with us to the Star Tavern after the gallery closes?" Miles asked. "You'll like the Star Tavern. They serve British ales and they even have stout. And wine."

"Interesting name," Fiona said.

"Yes, it's named after that Star Tavern in London."

"Very well. Sounds like fun. Could we ask the musician to go with us?" She nodded toward Luca Sutherland.

"Certainly. I don't know him, but I'll ask Cat to invite him." He approached Cat and whispered in her ear.

She grinned and nodded. Miles and Trevor went to the back of the gallery and resumed their argument quietly. After a few minutes, Cat made her way over to Luca, and she asked him to join them later. He agreed.

Thirty minutes later, the galley was closed and locked, Luca's violin was locked into Cat's storage room, and all the lights were turned off. Cat, Miles, Trevor, Fiona, and Luca Sutherland made their way on foot down Tombstone Canyon Road to the central part of the town known as Old Bisbee. Just before the group departed, Cat checked on the dogs. Tito was asleep on his bed, and Greta was watching the movie, "A Dog's Purpose." It was clear to Cat that Greta found this film very compelling. There were many dogs in the movie, and Greta was mesmerized, watching them with her ears perked up. Cat laughed softly as she closed the door behind her and joined the others.

***

Cat looked at their little group as they made their way to the Star Tavern. Trevor and Miles were again arguing about which "football club," that's what they called them, was the best in England. Luca was looking at Fiona and smiling. Fiona alternated between smiling at Luca and staring wide-eyed at colorfully-lit downtown Old Bisbee with its Saturday evening glittering lights and open shops, with tourists wandering the streets.

When they arrived at the Star, they found the tavern to be typical for a Saturday night. The tavern was full, customers and their drinks were at every table, and there was a lot of loud talk and laughter. Cat looked around and had a sudden strong feeling of missing her best friend and owner of the Star Tavern, Amanda. Amanda would be home again soon, Cat reminded herself, and she would be accompanied by her new husband, Ian Trevelyan. Cat sighed. Good. That means rowdy Greta will go back into their care. Cat would make sure that Ian understood how he really needed to push Greta's training. Greta's energy had to be directed into something more useful than tearing up pillows, jumping over the living room sofa and crashing into whatever was in her path, not to mention constantly pulling on the leash during walks.

Their group found the only empty table and gave their orders to a waiter. Cat noted that the waiter must be new because she'd never seen him before. He must be a Renata Romero hire, she thought to herself. Renata was the tavern's manager. She'd taken over when Amanda married Ian Trevelyan and began spending all her time with him. The new guy probably started after Amanda left with Ian for their European trip. And where was Renata? Cat didn't see her anywhere.

A few minutes later, Brett Jamison and his girlfriend Hannah West entered the tavern.

Cat waved them over. "Hey, Brett," she said. "Glad you joined us. Hi, Hannah. Good to see you again, too. When are you moving to Bisbee?"

"Glad you mentioned that, Cat," Brett said. He turned to Hannah and kissed her. "We're talking about her moving here. Sorry I didn't make it to the opening much earlier in the evening. Hannah and I…uh…got sidetracked." Hannah blushed and Brett grinned.

"Yes, I'd love to live here," Hannah said quietly. "We're trying to figure out how to make that happen."

Everyone made room for Brett and Hannah at their large round table. The waiter returned, and Brett ordered drinks for both himself and Hannah.

While they waited for their drinks, Cat looked around the dimly-lit room. She knew a lot of the people who were there enjoying themselves. They were mostly all locals. The exception was a woman and two men sitting at a table near the wall. The woman appeared to be in her mid-forties, and she was dressed in an expensive-looking dark suit and spike heels. The two men were in dark suits, too. Cat couldn't say why, but she knew immediately that the woman was in control. She was the boss and the two men were her…her what? Maybe body guards? What Cat was quite sure of, though, was that the woman was staring at the group around Cat's table. Or was she looking at just one person in their group? Cat knew it wasn't her but that's all she could say for sure. She just knew that the woman's gaze never left Cat's group. She had a serious look on her face, never smiling.

Cat's attention returned to her friends. They were all laughing now at some amusing story coming from Trevor. But the group's jovial atmosphere changed quickly when an older woman and a young man entered from the rear of the tavern's large, open room. Cat recognized the two as Renata Romero's mother, Consuela Romero, and Renata's boyfriend. What was his name? Cat asked herself. Memo? Yes, Memo. And where was Renata? Cat looked around. There were two young men behind the bar preparing and serving drinks, but Renata Romero still had not appeared. She was nowhere to be seen, which was very unusual for a Saturday night. For just a second, Cat remembered what Brett had told her earlier, how Renata had run away from the dead body in the street and about the man who had followed her briefly.

The older woman, Renata's mother, was wiping tears away with a tissue as she entered the tavern. She looked up and saw Miles, and she immediately came to his side. Cat wasn't surprised to see her go directly to Miles. Renata's mother was an excellent cook, she made dishes for tavern customers, and she had been giving cooking lessons to Miles on weekends They had become fast friends, both devoted to creating and serving the very best Sonoran cuisine.

"Oh, Señor Miles!" Consuela Romero began to sob.

"Señora, what's wrong?" Miles's voice and his face conveyed his concern. "Why are you crying?"

"My sweet child, *m'hija* Renata. She is missing. She has disappeared!"

4 Renata Romero

Cat reached across Miles to hand Señora Romero a tissue.

"*Gracias*," she whispered, struggling to contain a sob.

By this time, Miles had his arm around Señora Romero's shoulders. "What makes you think she's missing?"

The tall, dark-haired young man accompanying Renata's mother spoke. "Renata and I were supposed to have lunch together. I called her from Tucson a couple of days ago, and she told me that she had to work today. But we could eat lunch together and then meet after she got off work. But when I arrived, she wasn't here."

Miles stuck out his hand. "I'm Miles Trevelyan. And you are?"

"Sorry. My name is Guillermo Rojas. Everyone calls me Memo. I'm originally from Douglas, but I live in Tucson now because I'm a student at the University of Arizona. I just come home for weekends. Renata and I are…" Memo paused, "…we're serious about each other." He nodded his head to confirm what he'd just said. "It's not like her not to even show up. I tried calling her several times, but my messages always went to voice mail. So I called Señora Romero to see if she knew where Renata might be."

Miles turned to Señora Romero. "When did you last hear from Renata?"

"Thursday evening. She called me and said she and Memo would come to lunch at my house on Sunday. She said she was studying because she has a final exam."

"Renata is a student at Cochise College. I think that's what Amanda told me," Cat said.

"*Sí*, she is studying business," Señora Romero said. "She told me her exam was in accounting."

Memo spoke again. "We have no idea where she might be. The guys working here at the tavern don't know either. So we went upstairs to her apartment over the bar a few minutes ago. Someone has trashed the place, but there was no sign of Renata. We came down here to see if anyone had seen her."

Cat shook her head. "That doesn't sound very good. Have you called our police chief, Sam Morales?"

"I agree with Cat. I think you should call your copper," Miles said.

Cat frowned. She had suddenly remembered again what Brett Jamison had told her about seeing Renata early Friday morning, about the dead woman in the street, and about that strange man who chased Renata. She glanced over at Brett. He was frowning, too, no doubt thinking the same thing. Cat would definitely repeat to Sam Morales what Brett had told her about seeing Renata being chased.

"Yes," Memo said. He turned to Señora Romero. "I'm scared that she may have been kidnapped. I will call the police. You and I stay together, and we both will talk to the police."

Señora Romero nodded her agreement. She began to cry quietly.

Memo pulled out his phone and quickly reported Renata's disappearance. "The police will come quickly," he said.

"Let's go upstairs and take a look at Renata's apartment," Cat said. "Maybe we can see something that will give us a clue and tell us what's going on."

Brett stood up, too. "Hannah and I are going now. Cat, give me a call later about Renata. I'm concerned about her after what happened."

"I'll do that," Cat said.

Miles, Cat, Memo, and Señora Romero pulled away from the tavern table and headed upstairs.

"Trevor and Luca and I can wait here," Fiona said.

The four left the main room and trooped up the narrow stairs to Renata's apartment on the second floor. Cat led the way. She knew Renata's apartment well because it had been her friend Amanda's residence for many years.

Cat could see that the door to Renata's apartment was damaged. It appeared that someone attempted to pick the lock, and when that didn't work, the intruder took some kind of tool — a tire iron? a sledge hammer? — and smashed open the door. The outside wooden surface of the door had obvious damage, with splinters everywhere. Cat pushed the door open.

The interior of the apartment was a total disaster. Cat stepped in and gingerly picked her way past all the debris on the floor. She could see a couple of pots from the kitchen, broken dishes, and sheets and blankets stripped off the bed. There were books, too, and articles of clothing from the closet tossed around. Even her bathroom was trashed. The shower curtain had been ripped down and thrown on the floor.

The others followed Cat into Renata's apartment.

Señora Romero began crying again. "*Dios mío.*" My god.

"I'm calling Sam Morales. The police should be here," Cat said. She found her phone in her pocket. But before she could make the call, they all heard a siren in the street below. The sound seemed to be coming closer.

"I'll go see what's happening," Miles said. Memo and Señora Romero began picking things up off the floor and trying to find a proper place for them. Cat helped out, too. Señora Romero struggled to stop crying. Cat was keeping an eye out for anything unusual in the debris that might give them a clue about what had happened to Renata. She realized that the siren had stopped.

Only a couple of minutes later, Miles returned, accompanied by a new police deputy. Cat didn't know him. He was a tall, slender man, very fair with blond hair, dressed in the familiar Bisbee police uniform.

"This is Deputy Dave Chapman."

"Hi," Cat said. "I'm Cat Miranda. Where's Sam? And why was your siren on?"

"Ah," the deputy grinned. "So you're Cat Miranda? I've heard all about you. Chief Morales is on days now, and I'm on night duty. And I'm here because there was a fight out in the street. A couple of tourists who'd had too much to drink got into it. By the time I arrived, they were behaving better. They've gone their separate ways now."

"I'm glad you're here. We have a missing person to report," Cat said.

"Okay." Deputy Chapman pulled a notebook from his pocket. "Who are you two?" He gestured to Memo and Señora Romero. "And who is missing?"

"Renata Romero is missing," Memo said. "She's the chief manager of the Star Tavern, and this is Renata's apartment. I'm Renata's boyfriend, Guillermo Rojas, but everyone calls me Memo. And this is Renata's mother. I was supposed to eat lunch with Renata today, but she never showed up."

"What are you doing here?" Deputy Chapman asked. He looked at Cat.

"We're just trying to help," Cat answered.

"Yeah, Sam told me about you. He said you have a knack for sticking your nose into everything." He chuckled. "But he did admit that you've been helpful at times."

Cat frowned. She looked at Miles. He grinned and shrugged his shoulders.

Suddenly they all heard some yelling below in the alley behind the Star Tavern.

"What's that noise?" Deputy Chapman blurted out. He turned and headed back down the stairs. They all followed him.

The Star Tavern had a back door that led out into the alley. Near the back door was a small kitchen, a storeroom, and a staircase that led up Renata's apartment. Customers had to come in through the front door of the tavern because the back door that led to the alley was usually locked.

Deputy Chapman pushed open the back door and went into the alley. The others followed. They found two men crouching around the body of a young woman who was curled into a ball on the rough pavement. One of them looked up and said, "I called for help. They're sending an ambulance."

"Oh, no," Memo said. "That's Renata!" He stepped forward and crouched down to the young woman who was lying on the rough asphalt. She wasn't moving. He checked her pulse then looked up at Renata's mother. "She's alive, but she's not conscious."

"*Dios mío*," Senora Romero cried out when she saw her daughter. She fell to her knees and took Renata's hand in hers.

Deputy Chapman pulled out his portable police radio and made a call to his dispatcher at police headquarters, then a second call to confirm that the ambulance was on its way. He turned to the two men who had found Renata, and he told them to go stand under a single bare lightbulb which provided the backdoor's only harsh light.

"I need your names and identification," Deputy Chapman said. The two men began digging in their pockets for their wallets.

Cat guessed that they were in their mid-twenties. She heard one of them say, "We're sort of tourists. We've been to Bisbee several times. We came down from Phoenix for the weekend to hear some music. And maybe meet some chicks." She saw the young man look over at Renata and frown. "But not like this."

"Also, I'll need to know where you're staying and how to reach you. I need your cell phone numbers and your hotel number," the deputy added.

Cat and Miles approached Renata. Cat could see that Renata was completely unresponsive. There was only one shoe on her foot, a red sneaker. The other foot was bare, not even a sock. She was dressed in jeans and a pink t-shirt. Her clothing was rumpled and a little dirty, but not torn. She had no sweater or jacket.

Just at that moment, Señora Romero removed her own lightweight coat and placed it over Renata's upper body. At the same time, Memo removed his denim jacket, folded it up and placed it gently under Renata's head.

Renata groaned. Her eyelids fluttered for a moment, remained unfocused, then she passed out again.

Cat could hear the sounds of sirens approaching. Thirty second later, an ambulance pulled into the alley behind the Star Tavern.

Memo turned to Cat. "Señora Romero and I will go in my car to the hospital to be with Renata. Can you see that Renata's apartment is closed up as best you can? And tell the bartender downstairs what's going on? And tell him to keep people from going up to her apartment?"

"Yes, of course. Stay in touch, Memo. We're both concerned about Renata." To Cat, Memo looked very distressed.

Miles nodded his agreement.

Cat did just as Memo requested. They approached a young man, mid-twenties, polishing glasses behind the bar. The bartender introduced himself to Cat and Miles as Andy Edwards.

Andy said, "We've been worried sick about Renata. It's not like her to just disappear. We need her, too. She's our manager, and we rely on her."

"She's on the way to the hospital now," Cat said, hoping to reassure Andy. "They'll take good care of her. Meanwhile, her boyfriend Memo asked you to keep an eye on her apartment. Don't let anyone go to the back and go upstairs. The door is damaged and can't be locked so it would be easy to just walk into her apartment."

"No problem. I'll make sure no one goes up there. I can get someone in here tomorrow to fix the door and install a new lock, too. Please give me a call when you know something about Renata. All of us who work here will want to be kept in the loop."

"I'll do that," Cat said. Cat took a last look around the tavern. Nothing had changed except that the woman accompanied by two men was nowhere to be seen. Cat and Miles headed home.

Tito and Greta were ecstatic to see them.

"Come on, doggies. Let's go out and pee." Miles led them to the back door and opened it to the backyard. The dogs followed, tails wagging.

Not long after, Miles and Cat settled in their bed together, and Tito and Greta settled onto their large pillow beds.

"Cat, I've been wondering about something," Miles said.

"What?"

"Just before we went upstairs to Renata's apartment, Brett Jamison said something about…I don't know what…something. I'm not sure what he was talking about in reference to Renata. He said, 'after what happened.' What did he mean? What happened?"

"Oh, yeah. Remember when I said I had something to tell you about a dead woman? When Brett came into the gallery yesterday with a couple of paintings for me to hang, he was obviously upset. He told me that he was out walking early in the morning when he saw a woman go off the upstairs deck of the East-West Hotel and crash into the street head first. She ended up dead. He didn't know if it was a suicide or an accident or what."

"*Merde*. That's terrible."

"Yes. There's more. Renata was there, too, when this happened. She'd been jogging up Tombstone Canyon Road, and she was just across from Brett on the other side of the street. Brett said they waved to each other just before the woman came off the balcony. Then this dude came down from the second floor. But Brett said Renata had taken off running at top speed when she saw the dude coming down the stairs."

"*What?* Did she know him? Did this bloke catch her?"

"I don't know if she knew him or not. I thought maybe she realized he was coming after her because she'd seen him push the woman. But I don't know for sure. As far as catching her, Brett didn't think so. He said Renata was running fast, the man went after her but he gave up pretty quickly and came back. He disappeared after that. Brett said he ducked back into the doorway of the downstairs shop so this dude wouldn't see him. Then

Brett called an ambulance and Sam Morales. When the ambulance came, they took the woman's body away. After Sam talked to Brett and then him go, Brett went down to the Star Tavern to check on Renata. The Star was closed because it was still early. But he saw her light was on in her apartment upstairs, so he figured she was okay. He went home after that."

"So to the list of an accidental fall or an intentional suicide, we can add the possibility of a murder." Miles was frowning now.

"Yes. But we don't know if the dead woman has anything to do with Renata's disappearance. It just seems an odd coincidence. We'll have to wait until she's well enough to talk with us and tell us what happened. It's a mystery for now."

"A mystery?"

"Yes, a mystery."

"You like mysteries, don't you?"

"I do. I'm sort of like your dad. He likes solving mysteries, too."

"Yes, except that my dad is a retired copper, which means he's a trained and experienced police officer. You're a graphic designer and you run an art gallery. You are not a copper. And you're a tiny little thing. I don't want you to get into any trouble. I'm gone during the week so I can't be here to make sure you're safe."

Cat chuckled. "Okay. Then I'll keep my sleuthing to the weekends when you're here."

He made a face. "I know you'll do what you damn well please." He pulled Cat to him. "I love you, you know."

"I know, *querido*. I love you, too. I'll stay safe because I want the man I love to be happy."

"Good." Miles kissed her.

"What does *merde* mean, anyway?" Cat asked

"It's French for *mierdo*."

"Oh, of course. French. You're such a snob." She giggled again.

"Speaking French is not snobbery. Obviously, this means I'm going to have to kiss you to get you to shut up."

Cat could hear Tito's tail thumping against his big padded bed as Miles pulled her closer.

"Tito likes it when you kiss me." Cat giggled.

"Tito is a very smart dog. Now stop talking so I can kiss you."

5 Ted Yang

Cat and Miles were up early the next morning.

"I'll go start some coffee," Cat said. "Do you mind taking the dogs out to the backyard so they can do their business?"

"Certainly. I'll meet you in the kitchen."

Ten minutes later, Cat and Miles were sitting at their kitchen table sipping hot coffee. The dogs were lying on the floor a few feet away.

"What are you going to do today, Mr. Trevelyan?"

"Well, Ms. Miranda, I think I'll start the day with a long run, and I'll take Tito and Greta with me. I'll feed them when we return."

"Good. Maybe you can wear Greta out. She has an abundance of energy."

"Yeah, puppy energy. How old is she now?"

"I think about seven months. Or maybe eight months. I'll be glad when your dad and Amanda come home. Ian has a big job ahead of him training her. We were lucky with Tito. He's four years old and his previous owner obviously spent some time training him. He's very well behaved." She turned and spoke to Tito. "You're such a good boy, aren't you?"

At the sound of his name, Tito lifted his head and looked at Cat. His tail thumped against the kitchen floor.

"And what are you going to do today, Ms. Miranda?"

"I have a client coming in for a brief meeting this morning. His name is Ted Yang. He lives in Tucson now, but he's planning on permanently moving here to Bisbee. He told me he's going to open an art gallery in downtown Bisbee, and he wants some help with graphic design. You know — the regular stuff like a logo, website, social media, and some promotional material. We're just going to get started today. He's going to give me the basic info about the gallery, when and where, and all that. This afternoon, I'm going to call and see how Renata is doing. What's your plan for today after running the dogs?"

"I'm going to cook all day." Miles grinned.

Cat chuckled. "Who knew my nerdy history professor would like to cook so much?"

"I'm cooking for you and me and Trevor and Fiona. And probably baking, too. Also, I invited Luca Sutherland and Ana Hernandez. Luca seems like a nice guy. And his music is terrific. Ana is one of my favorite people. If I ever need a lawyer, I'm going straight to Ana."

"Okay. But I think you are really cooking for yourself, and we're lucky to get the benefit."

Miles shrugged. "True. I admit it. I get a lot of pleasure from the cooking and baking process."

"Why do you think you like to cook so much?"

Miles frowned. "I actually thought about that. I think it's because I used to cook with my mum when I was a little boy. I enjoyed that a lot."

"That makes sense."

"I'm thinking about writing a cookbook. Do you think I'm crazy?"

"No. I think you're irresistible."

Miles leaned forward and kissed Cat. "Why don't we ever argue about anything?"

"Because I'm right about everything and you always go along with me. What's to argue about?"

"Ah. So that's it. I guess that makes you irresistible, too." He kissed her again.

"Before you start cooking, I want you to come over and see this really cool little shelving unit that I just put in my office a couple of days ago. I potted some new plants in these pretty ceramic pots and placed them on the two shelves of the unit. The plants add a nice splash of green color in my office. I'm quite proud of the ceramic pots and the plants, too."

Just at that moment, Fiona entered the kitchen. "Good morning."

"Morning to you, too. Want some coffee?" Cat asked

"Oh, yes. Please. I'm kind of worn out from all the travel plus, last night when you two were dealing with the missing person problem, Luca and I took a long walk around downtown Bisbee. Trevor wasn't with us because he went to bed early so he could get up early and go birding. He left here early this morning, and I don't think he's come back yet. I'm glad you found Renata. Renata, that was her name? Is she doing okay?"

"Yes, I called her mum early this morning," Miles said. "Renata isn't seriously injured, but they're keeping her overnight tonight for observation, just to make sure she'll be all right. Señora Romero says she was drugged."

"Drugged? Goodness. Like a date rape situation?" Fiona asked.

"She wasn't raped," Miles said, "but I don't have any more details. I don't know why someone would drug her unless they were doing something illegal and she interrupted them. Or maybe she saw something that they didn't want her to see. I don't know."

Fiona nodded. "She'll tell you what happened when she feels better."

"So Luca wore you out hiking around Old Bisbee?" Cat asked.

"Yes, he pointed out all the sights and told me a little about the town's history. Very interesting place. I'm quite certain that I will be writing about Bisbee. There are several angles. There's the general travel-story approach, the art scene, the foodie scene, the old copper mine, and maybe a little history. I know a bit about the miners' strike in 1917 and how the strikers were kidnapped and deported on a train."

"Yes, that's called the Bisbee Deportation. Well over one thousand striking miners and their supporters were kidnapped and deported, shipped out by train into the New Mexico desert with no water or anything," Cat said. "The mining company didn't want them around stirring up more trouble with their strike."

"Fascinating. I want to explore some of the other neighborhoods, too. The way Luca described it, Bisbee is really a collection of villages that are all associated with each other."

"That's true," Cat said. "Typically we call them 'districts,' not villages. I'm going to fix us some breakfast. Then I suggest you come with me to my office above the art gallery. I have some maps for you to take with you that will help you figure out where all the districts are located. You'll probably want to start with Warren. That's where our hospital and schools are found. We're in Old Bisbee now, and there's Lowell and San Jose, too. And you'll probably want to go across the border to see Naco before you leave us. And you might want to take a tour of the old Copper Queen Mine."

"You can take my car rental," Miles said. "I'll be here in the kitchen all day."

"Thanks, Miles. I really appreciate that," Fiona responded. "Where do most of the residents live?"

"Everywhere. In all the different districts," Cat answered. She turned to Miles. "Do you want some breakfast?"

"No. We'll go for our run first." Miles stood and turned to the dogs. "Come on, beasties. Let's go." Before Miles finished talking, Greta was on her feet, tail wagging, ready to go.

Nearly an hour later, Cat and Fiona were still in Cat's office above the gallery. Cat had given Fiona several maps, brochures, and a booklet about Bisbee. Fiona put everything into her backpack along with a thermos of water. They were just finishing their conversation when suddenly the back door to the gallery opened, and Cat could hear Miles and dogs come crashing in.

"Here they come," Cat warned.

Fiona's eyebrows went up. "Noisy buggers, aren't they? And they are so big. I love them."

The two Great Danes bounded noisily up the narrow stairs to the second floor of Cat's art gallery. Miles was right behind them. Tito took a couple of steps toward the entrance to Cat's office and then stopped just outside the door. Miles stopped, too. Not Greta. She had too much momentum and too little coordination to come to a quick stop. She entered Cat's office at a run, but she immediately tried to stop her forward motion. She stretched her front legs out in front of her, paws first, trying to stop the slide across the polished wood plank floor. But it was too little too late. Greta slid all way across the small office and crashed into Cat's new shelving unit. The shelves swayed back and forth then fell over, and four pots fell to the floor. Three of them cracked open. Potting soil and plants spilled everywhere.

"*Oh!*" Cat gasped. She turned and yelled at the wayward dog. "*Greta!*"

Greta looked at Cat in dismay. She tucked her tail between her legs and crept away. She tried to hide behind Cat's small office desk, but she was too big. The desk began to wobble, and Cat's monitor and computer started to slide off the desktop and onto the floor.

Miles lurched forward and grabbed the monitor with one hand as he stabilized the computer with the other. But the desk itself began tipping over onto its side. A pile of papers, a small lamp, and a half-full coffee cup hit the floor, too. Fiona reached out and grabbed the computer from Miles before it hit the floor. Greta fled again, this time hiding behind a padded loveseat located in front of a tall bookshelf. She crouched down, trembling, a whine escaping her throat.

Fiona struggled not to laugh. Miles bent over, guffawing loudly.

Cat was furious. Tears filled her eyes. "When is your dad coming home? I can't take much more of this."

Miles managed to control himself and stop laughing. "Dad and Amanda will be back really soon. I'm going to help you clean up this mess before your client comes. Then I'll go cook. So cheer up, Cat. We'll fix this. I'm going to help you. You'll be back to normal in no time. And really, Greta didn't mean any harm."

"She's just a big lug that crashes into everything," Cat grumbled.

"Here," Fiona said. "I'm unplugging the computer and monitor. Let's put them over here so the spilled coffee doesn't get on them."

"Thanks." Miles lowered the computer to the floor.

Cat shook her head and sighed.

"How about if I take Greta off your hands for a while?" Fiona asked.

"Great idea," Miles said. "Let me feed and water them both first, and I'll find her leash. You can take Greta and keep her away from Cat for a while." He chuckled. "Tito can keep me company while I'm cooking."

"Thanks to both of you," Cat said. She glared at Greta who was cowering behind the loveseat.

Miles called the dogs, directed them down the stairs, and he followed. Before he closed the back door behind him, he called out, "Back in a minute."

Fiona found a rag in the bathroom and wiped up the spilled coffee. "This won't take long."

"Let's hope not. I have a client coming in about a half an hour. Thanks for taking Greta for a while."

"No problem. I love Greta. She just has a lot of puppy enthusiasm."

"That's a nice way of putting it." Cat frowned. "I think she's more like total puppy chaos."

About ten minutes later, Miles returned. "Fiona, Greta is downstairs. She has her leash on and it's attached to the stair railing so she can't come up here again. You can retrieve her there. I'm sure she'll be glad to see you. Here's the key to the car."

"Thanks, Miles. See you both later." Fiona waved goodbye and headed downstairs.

"Okay, Cat, let's start cleaning. I bet we can get your office nice and tidy really quickly. I'll reward you later for your diligence."

"Reward me?"

"Yes, when we get some kip. I mean a nap...or a siesta. Nice things will happen."

Cat laughed. "Nice things? That sounds interesting. Okay, let's get started."

~~~

Ted Yang arrived on time. Cat heard him ring the front door bell of the gallery. She hurried down to let him in.

"Hi, are you Ted?"

"Yeah, that's me. Thanks for seeing me on a Sunday. I couldn't make it yesterday, and really early tomorrow I'm going to Tucson to bring another load of my possessions. And it's back to Bisbee to meet a crew in the late afternoon. The crew will be cleaning up the new gallery space and doing some repairs and painting. On Tuesday, I check in with the repair and paint crew, and also I'm meeting with a sign maker to create a nice sign over the gallery door. Then back to Tucson in the evening."

"You're a busy guy. Let's go upstairs to my office."

"Oh, wow!" Ted breathed out. He was following her, but at the same time, he gazed with great interest at all the art on display in the gallery. "What terrific work!"

"All Bisbee artists," Cat said proudly. "Take your time."

Ted walked slowly around the room to get a better look at all the paintings and sculptures.

Cat watched him. He was a young man, maybe late twenties, slender, a little shorter than six feet tall, dark hair and eyes, and definitely of East Asian ancestry. His eyes had the classic epicanthal fold typical of all Chinese. He was dressed casually, in jeans and a light sweater.
~~~

"Okay. Thanks." Ted turned to her. "I hope to be living here soon so I'll be able to come to your openings. And I'll be able to return often to get a good look at all the art."

"So you're moving to Bisbee?"

"Yes, I already have an apartment rented. I'm staying there when I'm in town. The apartment is bare bones now, just a bed, a few clothes and a coffee maker. I just have to get all my stuff together and move it here from Tucson. Then I'll live here full time. Eventually I'll look for a house to buy."

"Moving is a lot of work. I don't envy you." As they were talking, Cat led him upstairs to her office.

"I'm getting rid of a lot of stuff first," Ted said.

"Smart move. Have a seat."

Ted sat in a chair next to Cat facing her computer. Everything was tidy and back to normal, just as Miles had promised.

"So you said you're opening a gallery?"

"That's right. I already have a gallery space rented. It's on Subway Street not far from the post office and the public library. The space was an art gallery for years, but the owner recently retired and moved back to southern California to be near his adult children. The real estate agent handling it is leasing it to me for six months. If everything goes okay, we'll start the process for me to purchase it. I'm taking a real risk, but I think it will pay off."

"Yes, I know the place. It's been empty for a few months."

"And it needs a lot of work. Clean up, repairs, painting and all that."

"I'm glad to see another gallery opening in Bisbee. The more galleries there are here, the bigger and better our reputation will be as an arts center. More people will come," Cat said.

"I've heard about you, Cat. Everyone says you have a great community spirit and you try to help out other artists. You have a great reputation. People say they can trust you."

"Oh, thanks, Ted. That means a lot to me."

"With that said, I'd like to tell you a couple of things that must remain between you and me. For a while anyway."

"Everything that goes on between me and my clients remains private between us."

"Great. The gallery isn't going to be your typical art gallery. It's going to be a specialized gallery of Chinese antiquities, plus some traditional, and even some contemporary, Chinese art."

Cat must have looked surprised.

"Yeah, not what you expected, huh?"

"No. Not at all," Cat said. "Tell me more."

"I have both an MBA and MA from the University of California at Berkeley. The MBA is in marketing and the MA is art history. I did the art history for love, and the marketing degree so I can make a living. My parents both came to the U.S. in the late nineteen seventies after Mao died and the Cultural Revolution was over. Deng Xiaoping began opening China to the outside world then. My dad is retired now, but he was an expert in ancient Chinese history, the Tang Dynasty to be exact. He and my mom were treated badly during the Cultural Revolution so they decided to jump ship when they had the chance. He ended up being hired as a history professor at Cal Berkeley. When they retired, they moved to Tucson. They have a house here in Bisbee, too, and often spend summers here." He paused. "Is all this family history boring you?"

"Certainly not," Cat said. "I've never known anyone with this kind of direct connection to China and these historical events. So you were born in the U.S.?"

"Yes, and that made me a U.S. citizen from day one. I grew up in California. But living with my parents meant I learned how to read, write, and speak Mandarin. My parents made it clear to me that they weren't going to allow me to lose my heritage."

"I get that. That's admirable, really."

"When I was in grad school, I came upon a lot of really interesting information about the art market in China. Later, I visited China several times and verified what I had learned here. The art market is way bigger than the U.S. art market. Bet you didn't know that."

"No, I didn't know that. In fact, all this is totally new to me."

"I've learned that the new elite, and by that I mean the super-rich Chinese citizens, are ardent art collectors. They started by buying traditional Chinese arts, and they still do."

Cat frowned. "I'm confused. What's this got to do with you?"

"Turns out a lot a lot of traditional Chinese art was taken out of China by Europeans and Americans at various times, mainly in the nineteenth and early twentieth centuries. Art and hand-crafted items were brought to the West. Some of it ended up in museums. But there's a lot of stuff that stayed in families, passed down from generation to generation."

"I didn't know about this."

"Have you ever seen that television show, *Antiques Roadshow*?"

"Sure."

"Then you've seen stuff like jade carvings, porcelain bowls, lacquer boxes, small statues of the Buddha, embroidered silk textiles, small paintings, and ink drawings. I'm talking about smaller items. Not the really big stuff that goes into museums. But even the smaller things can be worth several thousand."

"And the new Chinese elite want to acquire these cultural items and bring them back home to China."

"Exactly. After a while, many of these wealthy Chinese got interested in contemporary art, and some of them are collecting contemporary art now, too."

"You are focusing on traditional art? And you are the go-between?"

"Right. That's the idea. My job is to find the traditional arts and crafts in the U.S., and sometimes in Europe when it comes up for sale. The first part of my job is to find the art in North America, especially the U.S., or in Europe, and the second part is to sell that art to the Chinese. I've already conducted several deals. I plan to bring my finds to my gallery here in Bisbee to display it, and then do some serious marketing in China to sell the stuff. I'll do special exhibits in China, and I know that some of the Chinese elite will come here as well. I don't really expect to sell a lot to Bisbee tourists. But my website will show a legit gallery to potential collectors. The elite will see the art, want it, buy it, and I'll ship it to them. I'm hoping to eventually interest them in contemporary American art as well. Maybe they'll be interested in some Bisbee artists."

"Isn't it kind of hard to reach these rich elite?" All this was new to Cat.

"Not as hard as you might think. Weibo and WeChat are social media that are heavily used in China. Marketing on social media is common in China."

"And you can write and speak their language." She smiled.

"Right."

"But why make your headquarters in Bisbee? That, I do not understand."

"Here's the second part of my story. This part is a big secret."

"I won't tell." Cat was wide-eyed now, curious.

"I'm madly in love with your librarian."

Cat smiled. "What? The librarian at the public library? The Copper Queen Library?"

"Yes, her name is…"

"Jessica Weber. I know her. She's a sweetheart."

"Jessica Ming Weber. And yes, a real sweetheart."

"Ming? She has some Chinese heritage?"

"Right. Her mother is Chinese. Jessie's mom came to the U.S. in the 1990s for university studies, met Jessie's dad, they got married, and Jessie was born soon after. And then three more kids came on the scene. Jessie's dad owns a chain of car dealerships in the Los Angeles area."

Cat laughed. "A very American story. But why is your love for her such a big secret? Does she know you love her?"

"Yes, and Jessie loves me, too. But the problem is my parents. They want me to marry a traditional Chinese woman, some meek little Chinese girl that they choose and bring to the U.S. for me."

"An arranged marriage."

Ted nodded. "Right. I'm totally not interested in that. I'm an American of Chinese ancestry, not a Chinese man, and I want to find my own mate. I mean I already found my own mate. That's Jessie."

"They don't like her?"

"Liking or not liking isn't the issue. They just dismissed her. She's not Chinese. She's a half-breed, half Chinese and half American something. She's never been to China. She only knows a few phrases in Mandarin. She doesn't fit their profile."

"They sound pretty old-fashioned."

"Yes. So my plan is to open the gallery here and that means I'll get to spend a lot more time with Jessie. Also I can slowly introduce her to my parents in the hopes that they will come to accept her. I really hope they do accept her. But even if they don't, I'm marrying Jessie. She's the best thing that has ever happened to me."

"You have a big job ahead of you. Two big jobs."

"I do. But I'm excited and happy, and I can't wait to move to Bisbee and open my gallery."

Cat sat back in her chair. "Okay. Then let's get started. How about if I show you some websites, show you some of the options, see what you like, and then I'll be able to design something for you. We can set up a digital newsletter, too, to send out to potential collectors."

"I have some jpegs of some of the art I've already acquired and want to sell," Ted said.

"Excellent. I can use those."

Ted turned to the computer. "Yes, let's get started."

6 Greta's Calling

Following the maps that Cat gave her, Fiona decided to visit the district labeled 'Warren' first. She drove the rental car Miles had loaned her away from the town of Old Bisbee nestled among the Mule Mountains. She passed the Copper Queen Mine and immediately found herself in another one of the Bisbee districts, this one known as Lowell. Next, she navigated around a traffic circle and took an exit that would lead her into Warren.

Fiona immediately noticed a change. This district lacked the quaint nineteenth-century feel of Old Bisbee with its older homes and businesses in a narrow valley surrounded by steep mountainsides. Warren was much less mountainous, although not really flatlands either. She could see residential areas spreading out around the main Warren thoroughfare, known conveniently as Bisbee Road. Instead of the art galleries, shops, and nightclubs so common in Old Bisbee, the businesses in Warren trended more toward what you'd see in any town anywhere: a bank, a hardware store, a pharmacy. Almost immediately, she passed the Copper Queen Hospital which looked like a real medical center to Fiona. There was even a sign with an arrow labeled "Emergency."

Across the street from the hospital, a sign pointed to Bisbee High School. She passed a fitness center, a real estate agent's office, and a sign pointing to the Bisbee Farmer's Market. Best of all, there was even a Dairy Queen. Fiona had discovered Dairy Queen when she was in Phoenix for a brief time. The idea of ice cream popped into her head. Fiona decided that she needed some ice cream, and she would share it with Greta. Fiona concluded that Greta deserved a treat after having been yelled at and scared to death. The big Great Dane puppy sat calmly in the front passenger seat and watched the road.

"Want some ice cream?" Fiona glanced at Greta.

Greta wagged her tail.

"Okay. We'll get some in a few minutes."

Fiona drove all the way into Warren, past numerous homes along the side streets. Many were older homes with yards, some large and some small. She could see signs of gardens in some of the backyards. She saw several houses that could be classified as bungalows. In this case, quite a few were one and a half stories with the half story on the lower level. To enter the house meant walking up the front steps to a wide covered porch and to the front door. The lower level was more like a basement, often used for storage, or perhaps a laundry room. She could see very narrow windows just above ground level that allowed a little light into the lower level. In the case of the Warren homes, Fiona could see large doors that opened to allow a car to be driven in and parked. The lower level was, in effect, a car garage.

Having driven as far south as possible in the Warren district, Fiona circled the Warren Ball Park, which looked well used by local baseball teams. Now the road was leading her back to where she started. So Fiona went directly to the Dairy Queen drive-through and ordered two vanilla ice cream cones. The server at the window, a teenage girl, grinned and asked, "Are both of these for you? Or are you sharing?"

"Sharing, of course." Fiona smiled and wiggled her eyebrows.

The teenager giggled. "Good. I share with my dog, too. He likes strawberry best, but he won't turn away vanilla. I never give him chocolate because I heard that chocolate can make dogs sick."

Fiona nodded. "Yes, I read that chocolate is toxic for dogs. Giving them chocolate candy can even kill them. So Greta and I are sticking with vanilla."

"Greta? That's a great name."

"She's named after her mother, Greta Garbo."

The server laughed. "Awesome."

The cones came in a cardboard tray. Fiona sat the tray between her and Greta. She paid, waved goodbye to the server and drove forward. Greta was staring intently at the ice cream.

"Greta." Fiona said in a stern voice. Greta blinked and continued to watch the ice cream.

"Greta!" Greta looked up at Fiona. "No. Not yet." Greta whined. She drooled. She gaped at the ice cream. But she did not make a move.

"Good girl." Fiona headed back into Warren, turned left just past the hospital, then pulled off the road to park in an unpaved area just east of the hospital. She pulled the ice cream cones out of the cardboard tray. She held out one of the cones toward Greta. The ice cream cone disappeared down Greta's throat in one gulp.

Fiona laughed. She began licking her ice cream. Greta watched intently.

"Forget it, Greta. You had yours and this one is mine."

Greta whined. Fiona finished with her cone and gave the last bite to Greta.

"If you were my dog, I would be forced to spoil you."

Greta thumped her tail against the seat.

"Let's go take a walk." Fiona leashed Greta, they exited the car and began walking back toward the main road and the hospital. Fiona could see a small park-like area in the hospital's car parking area. It had trees, grass, and a couple of concrete benches. Fiona could see a little girl in a wheel chair there. Next to her on one of the concrete benches was a woman with blonde hair pulled back into a ponytail. She was dressed in a uniform. Maybe a nurse?

The little girl squealed and pointed to Greta. A big smile on her face told Fiona that the little girl wanted to meet Greta. The woman looked at Fiona and smiled. Fiona could see the question on her face.

Fiona and Greta walked over to the pair.

"Would you like to meet this dog?" Fiona asked. She glanced at the woman. Yes, she was a nurse. Fiona could see her name tag: June Tyner, R.N. To Fiona, the nurse, June, looked to be in her late twenties. She was very pretty.

The nurse nodded, smiling broadly.

"Yes! Please!" The little girl giggled. "What's its name?"

"This is Greta. She's a girl. She's a Great Dane."

"I know," the girl said. "I know all the dog breeds. She's what they call a Harlequin Great Dane."

"Really? What does that mean?" Fiona asked. She noticed immediately that the little girl was extremely thin and pale, a very sick child.

"See how she's mostly white but with all those black patches? They call that Harlequin." The girl looked up at Fiona and spoke with authority.

"Oh, that's good to know. Greta is young. She's still a puppy."

By this time, Greta had approached the little girl. Fiona watched carefully, her grip tight on the leash. She didn't know what Greta would do. Much to her relief, Greta placed her head directly on the little girl's lap. Her tail was wagging slowly as she gazed up into the girl's eyes.

"Oh, look! Greta loves me. And I love her." The child stroked Greta's head repeatedly.

"I'm Fiona. I'm visiting from England. Greta actually belongs to some friends who live in Old Bisbee. Greta and I are taking a sightseeing tour of Bisbee."

"I'm June Tyner. I'm a pediatric nurse here in the hospital. I just started working here. This is Mia, and she's a patient here at the hospital. We decided to come outside and get a little fresh air and sunshine."

"I have leukemia." Mia looked directly at Fiona.

"Oh." Fiona didn't know what to say to that. She decided to stick with dogs as a topic of conversation. "Do dogs make you feel better?"

"Oh, yes!" Mia answered. "Much better." She leaned forward and kissed the top of Greta's head. Greta responded by licking Mia's face several times.

Mia giggled and kissed Greta again.

"Looks to me like you have a therapy dog in the making," June said.

Fiona's eyes went wide. "Oh. Really? Of course. I never thought of that. Yes, it does seem she could be a good therapy dog."

"She'll need some training, but it looks to me like Greta is well on her way. Dogs can have a calling, just like humans do. I think being a therapy dog may be Greta's calling."

"June, would you like to come to dinner this evening? My friend has invited me so I'll have to ask if you can come, but I think he'll say yes."

"Sure. I just moved here and started this job. I'd love to meet some of the Bisbee residents. I only know a few people who work in the hospital. I can tell you more about the dog training then. My cousin trains therapy dogs."

"Really? Here in Bisbee?"

"No. In the Los Angeles area. But he might be able to get you started with good information."

"Okay, give me a minute." Fiona handed the leash to June. She walked a few steps away, found her phone and called Miles. When she returned and took the leash again, she said, "Miles says yes. Consider yourself invited. I can text you the directions and the time we'll meet for dinner." June gave Fiona the number to text, and the task was completed.

Just then the double doors to the hospital opened and a woman called out. "Okay, Mia. It's your turn."

"We have to go for Mia's treatment," June said. "But while you're here, I suggest you go over to the geriatrics wing of the hospital. Try Greta out on some of the older folks. They often respond very well to therapy dogs." She pointed in the direction of the geriatric wing.

Fiona waved goodbye to Mia and June and followed June's directions. She found three elders outside, all sitting in their wheel chairs, enjoying the winter sun. Greta reacted to the elders in exactly the same way she had reacted to Mia. She went from one person to another and placed her head in their laps. She was received with great warmth and affection.

After about half an hour of "therapy," Fiona wasn't sure who was benefiting more, the geriatric patients or Greta. It was clear that Greta was a dog who benefited from a lot of love and affection.

"Okay, Greta. Let's head back to Cat's place. We're learned a lot today. I'm going to enjoy telling them about your therapy skills."

When they arrived at Cat's house, Fiona leashed Greta but, instead of going into the house, she headed off down the street with Greta prancing at her side.

"Let's take a little walk, Greta. I saw something interesting on that side street that we passed back there. Let's go take a look."

~~~

Mari Spencer hit the nail into the wooden fascia board with a sure aim. It was the last nail, and now the fascia board was part of a lovely covered deck attached to the side of a large home on a narrow street in Old Bisbee. There was a glass door in the home's dining room that led out to the deck. She turned around and looked at her part-time helper, Luca Sutherland. He was shirtless, carrying two buckets of paint toward the house from Mari's truck on the street.

"Aren't you cold?" Mari looked at him sideways.

"Nah," Luca replied. "It's sunny today and pretty warm. And I'm working hard."

"Well, you'd better get a shirt on or you'll have all the women in Bisbee gathering to check out your abs." The look on her face was best described as a smirk.

Luca chuckled. "I doubt my abs would be of much interest to any woman."
~~~

"Oh, yeah?" Her eyebrows wiggled and she made a gesture behind Luca.

He turned and saw Fiona Davis standing next to Mari's truck. In her hand was the leash and Greta was waiting patiently on the other end of it.

"Oh. Hi, Fiona," Luca said.

Fiona looked up at Mari, a grin on her face. "You're quite correct. The scenery here is lovely."

Mari laughed. "Yeah, I get that. But I don't pay Luca to look good. He has to paint these new fascia boards before the day is over. I'm Mari Spencer, by the way."

"Fiona Davies. I'm visiting from England. Why are you two working on a Sunday? Is that typical here?"

"Hell, no," Mari said. "But it couldn't be helped. We have to get this job finished before the owners show up, and that's going to be tomorrow. Probably. I'm not sure, but I can't take a chance. I want it finished today." She turned to Luca. "I should have said this before. Thanks, Luca, for agreeing to work today."

"Not a problem."

Fiona took a step back. "I'm just walking the dog. I guess I'd better get going."

"See you this evening?" Luca asked.

"You will?"

"Yes, Miles invited me to dinner. He told me you'll be there."

"Yes, I'll be there." Fiona felt a sudden wave of pleasure. She liked Luca. She liked him a lot. She realized she was just standing there. Both she and Luca had fallen silent, looking at each other and smiling.

"Brilliant," Fiona finally said.

Luca grinned. "Yeah, brilliant. Okay, see you later." He turned to continue carrying the buckets of paint to the new deck.

Mari and Fiona exchanged grins.

"Nice meeting you, Mari." Fiona waved.

"Yeah, you too, Fiona. See you around."

Fiona turned to Greta and reached out to stroke the big puppy's head. She was rewarded with a tail wag and a lick on her hand. "You're such a sweet girl. Come on. Let's go home."

Fiona and Greta continued their walk back to Cat's house. Fiona chatted as she walked, and every time she said something, Greta wagged her tail. "Luca has nice abs, don't you think? And chest and shoulders and other parts, too. He's handsome, too. That face. So nice. " Greta wagged her tail again.

7 Chef Miles

The sun had already set when Miles and Cat's guests began to gather for dinner. Trevor was back from another birding trip, and Fiona had returned in mid-afternoon with Greta. A knock at the door brought Ana Hernandez and June Tyner, both of whom had arrived at the same time. Finally, Luca arrived, carrying his violin in its case.

"You seemed to like the music I played at the gallery opening so I thought I'd bring my violin in case you want to hear more," Luca said to Cat. "But only if you're interested. I don't want to be intrusive."

"Intrusive? No way. Hearing you play again would be great," Cat said. "We all love your music. You play the violin really well."

"Thanks. Actually, I play several instruments. My favorite is cello. I just hope I don't make the coyotes howl. I did that a couple of nights ago. I was playing outside in the garden of the one of the restaurants up one of the Bisbee side streets. The coyotes sang along."

Cat laughed. "Yeah, they are big on singing along. The Native Americans call them 'song dogs' for a reason."

"Oh, I'd love to hear a coyote," Fiona said. "We don't have coyotes In England. I've never seen one, much less heard one. I'm in London most of the time."

"I can fix that," Cat said. She found her phone, clicked on a website and turned up the volume. She handed the phone to Fiona.

Fiona pressed the video play button and a few seconds later, the coyotes began loudly yipping and howling. "Blimey!" Fiona's eyes were wide. "Amazing."

Suddenly a low moaning sound came from the kitchen. The sound increased in volume and pitch until the low moaning sound transformed into a loud howl.

Miles stuck his head around the kitchen door. "Hi, everyone. That's Tito. He's singing along."

They all laughed. Tito took a breath and continued howling.

"I guess I better turn this off," Cat chuckled. "We don't want to disturb the neighbors. Or listen to Tito singing all night."

Tito appeared and came to stand next to Cat. "Everything is okay, my little Chiquitito. There are no coyotes here." As she stroked his head and ears, she looked around the living room. Greta was crouching behind the sofa, trembling. "Look, Fiona." She pointed to Greta.

"Poor baby," Fiona said. She went to Greta, caressed her and spoke to her in a comforting voice. "You're okay. All is well. You're safe."

"I could use some help getting the table set," Miles called from the kitchen.

"Coming," Cat said.

In only a few minutes, the table was set and Miles started carrying plates and bowls full of food from the kitchen to the dining room table. Cat lit candles, poured the wine, and everyone took a seat.

"Miles, please introduce us to all this beautiful food," Cat said. She could see that Miles was having a really good time. She thought to herself that he must really, really like cooking. And sharing it with everyone, too.

"Thank you, Señorita Miranda. I'll tell you about each dish, what's in it and all that. Then, when we're finished eating, I would like it very much of each of you introduce yourself and tell us all something about you."

Everyone agreed.

"Okay, first, I have an appetizer, guacamole, of course. Next comes some *sopa,* or soup in English, chicken tortilla soup. And we have a big salad, *ensalata.* And a big bowl of *pico de gallo* to put on anything and everything. And on the platters, you'll find *fajitas, tacos, chimichang*as, *quesadillas,* and some *nopalitos* on the side. And some *queso panela* on this little plate. Eat it as is or put it in your salad. And we have flan and *helado* for desert. Is there anyone here who doesn't know at least a little bit of Spanish?"

"Cor, Trevelyan! Have you been cooking for days?" Trevor asked.

"No. Just today. All day."

Trevor looked around. "I guess I'm the only one who doesn't speak Spanish. I had to take French and German in school, but I can't speak either one. I am learning some Spanish, though. It's impossible not to do so here in Arizona. I have a dictionary on my smart phone."

"We'll help you out," Miles said. He began ladling out soup into each bowl. "This chicken tortilla soup is a classic."

Ana Hernandez nodded her head. "Especially good for cold winter evenings. *Mi abuela* makes this often."

Miles turned to Trevor. "Her grandmother makes this."

"*Abuela.* Yes, I'm learning Spanish," Trever said. He turned to Ana and smiled.

They all dug in. Throughout the meal, Miles Trevelyan received great praise for his culinary efforts.

~~~

"Now that we're all really stuffed, let's all introduce ourselves, as Chef Miles has requested," Cat said.

No one said anything.

"Oh, don't be shy," Cat said.

"I'll go first," Fiona said. "Then I'd like for June to be next."

"Whoo-hoo," Cat smiled. "Fiona first!"

"My name is Fiona Davies. I'm English and a loyal subject of the Queen. For the record, I'm an anti-monarchist which means
~~~

I think we should do away with the monarchy. It's an antiquated and very expensive institution, and I believe we can do without it. But I love Queen Elizabeth so I'm for keeping her."

"My sister has opinions," Trevor said, smiling.

"I was born in London, and I've lived most of my life in London. I'm a city girl. I have two little brothers." She gestured to Trevor sitting across from her. "Trevor is one of my annoying little brothers."

Trevor grinned and nodded.

"I'm a writer. I read English literature at university. I started writing at an early age. After college, I worked on the staff of an online magazine devoted to the arts. I also started freelancing around that time. Unfortunately, the online magazine folded. The editors just couldn't get enough money together on a reliable basis to continue publishing and also pay the staff. So I went freelance. I've been doing that for three years now."

"What kind of freelancing do you do?" Cat asked.

"To keep myself afloat, I write articles for different businesses. Most of the bigger businesses have a website with blogs. I write their blogs on exciting subjects like new software for industrial tool production. Or best marketing strategies for video-game companies. Then, when I can save up enough money, I hit the road and write about whatever I see and do."

"Like a trip to the American Southwest?" Ana asked.

"Yes, exactly. I also went to Mexico City this time around. I have plenty of material for articles on tourist destinations, as well as special topics like food…"

"Sonoran cuisine!" Miles interrupted.

"Yes. I hope to talk to you about that very subject, Miles."

"Do you still write about the arts?" Luca asked.

"Yes, I've profiled artists, writers, musicians, theater companies, arts centers, and more. I'm hoping you'll allow me to interview you while I'm here." She looked at Luca and smiled.

Much to Fiona's surprise, an odd expression had appeared on Luca's face. Not pleasure, not embarrassment, not shyness. What was it? Fear? Could she be right about that? Was that the shadow of fear that passed over his handsome face? No, she decided it wasn't fear. Maybe sadness. Yes, he appeared to be sad. Why would an interview request make him sad? There has to be a story there, she said to herself.

Returning to her freelance writing jobs, Fiona said, "Another topic I'm thinking about is how to recognize if your dog has a calling to be a therapy dog."

"What? What are you talking about?" Trevor asked.

"So it's like this. I recently met this big, beautiful Great Dane puppy, and her name is Greta."

Cat nodded and smiled.

"Greta is almost full grown. But she's still a puppy in terms of understanding how to move around. She doesn't realize how clumsy she still is. Just this morning, Greta accidentally wrecked Cat's office."

Cat rolled her eyes.

Fiona looked at Cat and said sweetly, "Greta is deeply regretful for causing so much havoc. She didn't mean to knock over your plants and break your pots, and she certainly didn't mean to almost destroy your computer and monitor."

Everyone laughed, except Cat, who shook her head and grimaced.

"So Greta went with me to visit Warren. That's one of the Bisbee districts, Trevor. We drove around first then we got some ice cream."

"We?" Miles asked, grinning now.

"Yes, we. Greta needed some cheering up after her traumatic morning. Ice cream was perfect for that. She and I both prefer vanilla flavor. Then we went for a walk, and that's where we met June outside the hospital. She was with this little girl named Mia who is very sick. Mia told me she has leukemia."

June nodded. "Mia is not doing very well despite our best efforts to care for her. I worry about her."

"Mia fell in love with Greta, and Greta loved her back," Fiona continued. "They traded kisses, and Greta put her head in Mia's lap for the entire time we were there. June recognized that Greta could very well become an excellent therapy dog. At her suggestion, we also visited some of the geriatric patients, too. They also were drawn to Greta, and she was very loving in return. In every case, she went up to the patient, put her head in their lap, looked up at them with love in her eyes, and she wagged her tail every time."

"Yes, my cousin in Pasadena…that's in the Los Angeles metro area…trains therapy dogs," June explained. "He told me that many dogs often have a calling from birth to do something special in their lives. K-9 dogs are an example of that. And sniffer detection dogs. That's usually the case with therapy dogs, too. From early on, they have an amazing ability to detect when someone is upset or lonely or needing a little affection. These dogs try to give that to the person needing it. Greta is obviously that kind of dog."

"Oh," said Cat. "Oh…oh…"

"What?" Miles asked.

"I think Greta has been trying to give me some therapy. When I feel really sad, she comes and puts her head in my lap."

"Why do you feel really sad?" Miles asked. A look of real concern passed over his face.

"Because you're not here. We were together for six months traveling all over Europe. We were together all day and all night for months. Then we returned home, and now you're only here part of the time. I really miss you when you go to Tucson."

"Oh, Cat," Miles groaned. He got up and went to her. He hugged and kissed her. "I'm so sorry. I'll be here all of December and part of January on the university's Christmas and New Year's break."

"Oh, I'm being silly," Cat said. "Don't listen to me. But I'm really glad you'll be here."

Cat looked at Greta. "Come here, baby." Greta came to Cat, put her head in Cat's lap, and wagged her tail. "Okay, Greta, you and I are going to be friends from now on," Cat said, as she stroked Greta's head. "But I think you'd better stay out of my office."

"Hey, Trevelyan," Trevor said. "I have an idea. Want to make your woman happy? Give up that university professor job. Move to Bisbee full time and open a restaurant or a catering service."

Miles laughed. "And write a cook book, too? I'm thinking about it."

Cat was surprised. She decided to ask him later if he was just joking or even a little bit serious. She didn't know what to think.

Fiona spoke up. "And while you are considering these things, also think about getting Greta some training and make her available as a certified therapy dog." She glanced over at Luca. He was watching her, but when her eyes met his, he turned away. That same sad expression was on his face.

"Yes," June added. "Therapy dogs really are needed, not only for sick people but whenever there's any kind of tragic event. The dogs help people deal with distress, anxiety, and depression. My cousin told me once that Great Danes make wonderful therapy dogs."

"I'll talk to my dad about this when he and Amanda return," Miles said. "I'm sure he'll be interested."

"Okay. June, you're up next," Cat said.

"Well, you already know a lot. I grew up in southern California. I started my work life as a nurse there. I went back to school to specialize in pediatrics and that's where I met my husband. I mean my ex-husband. We were married for a couple of years, but it was clear almost from the beginning that we were *not* meant for each other. When we got divorced, I decided I needed a big change. I wanted to get away from LA so I started looking for a job in a small town in a sunny climate and not more than a day's drive from my family. Bisbee came up. I applied and I got the job. I've only been here a couple of months. Thanks for inviting me. It's so nice meeting all of you."

"What do you do for fun?" Trevor asked.

"I like to do nature photography."

"Really? Do you photograph birds?" He was interested.

"Yes, definitely."

"Brilliant!" Trevor grinned. "Let's go out together. You take photos and I'll watch. The birds, I mean, not you. I'll watch the birds. I didn't mean watch you."

Miles laughed. "Sure. Right."

"Sounds like fun," June replied.

"Trevor, since you're talking," Cat said, "how about if you go next?"

Trevor nodded. "I'm Trevor Davies, and that's my annoying big sister Fiona."

Fiona blew him a kiss.

"I'm an environmentalist, a conservationist, and an ornithologist. That means I'm a bird nerd. I was working for an enviro group that merged with a larger group. I just got news early this morning that the merged environmental group has found funding now to keep me in my position. So I can go home anytime and start work again."

"And what do you do for fun?"

"I love football. I like to play, I like to watch, and I have favorite teams. I love everything about football."

"He means soccer," Miles explained. "And Trevor is totally clueless about which teams are the best."

Ana smiled. "My team is the best."

"You play football…uh…I mean soccer?" Trevor asked.

"Actually, I'm the coach of a girls' team. They are all eleven and twelve year olds. Our team's name is the Douglas Demons."

"Can I come and watch you play?" Trevor asked.

"Sure. Maybe you can give us some tips from an English perspective?"

"Brilliant. I'd be delighted."

"Keep going, Ana," Cat said. "What else do you do beside coach little demons?"

"I grew up in Douglas, which is a town on the border near Bisbee. It only takes about half an hour to drive over there. My mom and siblings still live there, so I go home often to see them and to coach the girls' team. My dad passed away several years ago. Most of the time, I'm in Bisbee working. I'm an attorney in partnership with Jeremy Flores. He and I handle all kinds of cases so it's never boring. We stay busy, too. There's always plenty of work."

"Ana is very well-informed," Cat said. "She's been of great help to us all. Plus, she's a real sweetie."

Ana smiled. "I like Cat because she has a gift for stumbling across some very interesting mysterious situations that typically involve some kind of crime. And she's a sweetie, too."

"Luca?" Cat looked at him and smiled.

"I don't have a lot to tell. I was living in central Mexico. I graduated from Universidad Nacional Autónoma de México. I decided I needed a change, sort of like you, June, though no marriage was involved. So I came north. I crossed *la frontera* at Nogales. Then I saw an ad for a job here in Bisbee doing handyman work. I applied and now I work for Mari Spencer. Also, I started doing gigs playing music. I've been in Bisbee about a year, and I really like it here." He paused, but only for a couple of seconds. "That's all. Cat, you're next."

Fiona was acutely aware that Luca had told them very little about himself. She wanted to know more.

Cat spoke next: "Oh, everybody knows me. I was living in Phoenix and came home to take care of my brother Luis. He was very ill, and when he died, I moved back home permanently. I took over his art gallery, and I started my own graphic design business. Miles?"

"I'm Miles Trevelyan. I'm an assistant professor history at the University of Arizona in Tucson. I like to do historical research. I like writing books about history. And I like to cook. Most of all, though, I like Catalina Amalia Miranda. Like as in love."

"How did you meet?" Fiona asked.

"Cat threatened to beat me up with a baseball bat." Miles grinned.

"You were trying to break into my house!" Cat shot back, giggling.

"No, I wasn't! I had a key. Remember?"

Cat turned to Fiona. "It was all a big misunderstanding. I let him stay the night in what is now my office. That was a good thing because, later that night, this bad guy broke in and Miles fought him off."

"That bloke hit me, and I was bleeding over my eye, so after I chased him off, Cat sat me down, cleaned my wound and put a bandage on it. That turned out to be really nice for me because she had on this really thin nightgown, the night was cold, and I could see her …"

"Shut up!" Cat said.

Everyone laughed.

"Maybe it's time for some music in the living room," Fiona said.

"Before we do that, could I ask something?" Ana looked around the table at everyone. "I'd like to know more about this woman who ended up dead on Tombstone Canyon Road. I've heard a bunch of rumors. Cat, know anything about that?"

"Not much, Ana. I'll tell you what I know, but let's agree to not talk about this to anyone, okay? I have some information from Brett Jamison that's not common knowledge. I don't know if he wants anyone to know what he saw." She looked around the table. Everyone nodded their assent.

Cat quickly told them what Brett had told her: seeing and greeting Renata Romero early in the morning, the woman's body suddenly coming off the balcony of East-West Hotel along with a big piece of pottery, a man dressed in an ivory-colored suit coming down from the balcony and chasing Renata, then losing her, and Brett holding back, hiding beneath the balcony so he wouldn't be seen by the man in the white suit.

"Has the dead woman been identified? Do you think Renata's disappearance has something to do with this?" Ana asked. "And how is Renata, anyway? I heard that she was taken to the hospital."

"I don't know if there's a connection between the dead woman and Renata, but I'm going to try to find out. Tomorrow, I'll do my best to talk to her. And Sam Morales, too."

"Who is Sam Morales?" Fiona asked.

"Our police chief. He's a friend," Cat answered. She turned to Ana. "Sorry. That's all I know."

"Well, let's stay in touch. I have this feeling that there's something bigger going on. I want us all to stay safe." Ana grinned. "And someone may need an attorney before this is all over."

They all chuckled.

"Let's go sit in the living room," Cat said. "Luca is going to play for us."

~~~

They all made themselves comfortable in the living room, and for nearly an hour, Luca played his violin. Sometimes he played solos of both classical European music and traditional Mexican folk tunes, and sometimes he played folk songs that they all knew. They sang along as he played. Their time together was relaxed and very pleasant.

"Time for me to go," Luca finally said to everyone. "Thanks so much for listening to the music." He put his violin in its case and stood up. "I'm supposed to meet Mari Spencer early tomorrow for a job. I have to do some painting on that house we're working on."

"Thanks, Luca. That was great hearing you play," Cat said. "Yes, thanks, Luca," the others said.

Luca said goodbye to everyone and headed out the door. Fiona followed him onto the front porch.

Luca put his violin case inside a large backpack he'd left on the front porch earlier. He slipped the backpack on.

"Want a ride home?" Fiona asked.
~~~

"No, I came on my bike. I'll go home on my bike."

"What about that interview I asked you about?"

Luca turned to face her. He put his hands on Fiona's shoulders. "Fiona, you're so beautiful and so smart. And the first time I heard you speak, that English accent of yours, I knew that I wanted desperately to kiss you." He pulled her close and kissed her gently on her lips. Then kissed her again. And again. "And you smell good, too."

Fiona felt herself responding to his kisses. She realized that this was what she'd wanted all along – for Luca to kiss her.

Luca pulled away. "But you don't want to get mixed up with me," he said. "I'm nothing but trouble."

Ten seconds later, Luca Sutherland was on his bike, heading down the street toward Tombstone Canyon Road.

Fiona stood there, stunned. What just happened? What does he mean that he's nothing but trouble? She watched him disappear into the night. It wasn't until she couldn't see him anymore that Fiona realized Luca had never answered her question about an interview.

8 In the Way

The next morning, Fiona woke up later than usual. It was almost nine when she went into the kitchen for some coffee. She found Cat at the kitchen table drinking a cup and looking at text messages on her cell phone. Tito was on a pillow in the corner.

"Hey, Fiona. How's it going?" Cat asked.

"Good. I slept well." She poured herself a cup of coffee and sat at the table.

"Thanks so much for straightening me out about Greta. Now I know how to deal with her. I'll keep her out of my office until she gets better control of her gangly self. And now I definitely want to learn more about therapy dogs. I'm sure Ian and Amanda will be interested in that."

"My pleasure. Greta is a real sweetheart. Where is she anyway?"

At that moment, Miles came into the kitchen with Greta. He was red in the face and his t-shirt was wet with sweat. Greta was panting. She headed to the dogs' water bucket, and she began to drink noisily.

"Greta and I ran fast and hard this morning. That took some of the buzz out of her. Maybe she'll take a nap now. As for me, I'm going to take a shower." Miles disappeared into the bedroom he shared with Cat.

"I've been wondering, Cat." Fiona looked at Cat, a question on her face.

"About what?"

"I've been thinking about what Ana Hernandez asked you last night. I'm talking about the woman who went off the balcony into the street. It seems kind of strange that no one knows who she is. I have the impression that everyone in Bisbee knows everyone else."

"That's pretty much true. But we get a lot of tourists here. The dead woman may have been a tourist. I talked briefly this morning to Sam Morales, our police chief. He said that she had no identification on her. No one has been reported missing locally. So the police are now looking at a larger database of missing persons, starting with the states of Arizona and New Mexico. If they don't find her there, they will look on the national level. He said he also checked with the East-West Hotel staff. They gave him the name of the man in the white suit who had been staying there, but he's already checked out. He paid cash for the room. Sam said he doubts that the guy gave his real name. Sam can't find anything on him either. He's a mystery, too."

"And what about that pot that was thrown off? Was it connected to the woman?"

"I don't know, but I'm going to try to find out," Cat replied.

"Maybe Renata can shed some light on this. If she can identify the person or persons who drugged and kidnapped her, then maybe a connection could be made to the dead woman," Fiona said.

"I hope she can remember. She was seriously drugged." Cat paused. "Fiona, you strike me as a very observant person."

"It's the writer in me. I'm always looking for details for a story." Fiona smiled.

"When Miles and I went upstairs to Renata's apartment with her boyfriend and mother, did you notice anything peculiar in the tavern after we left? Were you approached by anyone? Did anyone try to follow us? Did you overhear anyone saying anything about Renata's disappearance?"

"No. Not really. Those people who had been watching us were still there. They didn't move."

"Watching us? Do you mean the two men and the woman over in the corner? I noticed them, too. They aren't locals and they didn't look like tourists," Cat said.

"Yes. Exactly. The woman was in the corner in the dark, and the two guys sat around the same table but a little forward as if they were there to protect her," Fiona said.

"My sense is that the woman was sitting back in the shadows so she couldn't be easily seen or identified. She looked like she's maybe in her late forties or early fifties. She never smiled once. Neither did the two guys."

"And it looks like she has money. Her clothes and jewelry advertised her affluence," Fiona added.

"Those two guys maybe were her bodyguards?" Cat asked.

"Yeah, that's what it looked like to me. But why were they watching us?"

"I have no idea. And I don't think it was our entire group. I've been thinking about it since that night. I think they may have been focused on Luca," Cat added.

Fiona frowned. "Luca? I wonder what that's about. What do you know about Luca?"

"Not much, really. There's this woman here in Bisbee named Mari Spencer who has a home renovation service. She does a lot of carpentry, too, adding porches on houses, replacing windows, and other jobs like that. She's very good. I've hired her several times to work on the gallery and on my house, too."

"Yes, I met Mari briefly."

"Nearly a year ago, Mari showed up with Luca to do a job for me. Mari introduced him as her part-time employee. They went right to work. In fact, they've been here to work maybe three times since then. But I've never had a chance to talk much with Luca. I've seen him play music around town, and I hired him to play at my last opening. We're friendly, but I don't know him very well at all."

"Lots of little bits and pieces of information, but nothing fits together." Fiona frowned.

"That's the fun part, fitting all the pieces together," said Cat.

Miles returned, now showered, dressed and ready to go. He came around the table and kissed Cat. "I'm off to Tucson. I have some paperwork I have to complete this afternoon, turn in this last semester's grades, and I have a departmental meeting tomorrow morning. I'm going to try to track down my dad, too, and find out when they plan to return. I learned from the last email I got from him that he and Amanda were exploring the Shetland Islands, off the north coast of Scotland."

"I tried to call Amanda, too, but I couldn't get through to her. The Shetlands? That's crazy. It's winter and they went to some islands in the North Sea!" Cat said. "They should go somewhere warm."

"I think so, too, but their trip there has something to do with birds. They're looking for gannets and fulmars." He shrugged his shoulders. "Don't ask. I don't have a clue. All I know is that gannets and fulmars are birds."

"Are you planning on telling your dad about what's going on here? This dead woman and Renata?"

"No. I don't see any point in it. They can't do anything about it. And they'll just worry."

"That's what I think," Cat said. "If I manage to reach Amanda, I won't mention all this."

"So, Cat, I'll be home tomorrow afternoon. Do you want anything from Tucson?"

Cat returned his kiss. She liked it a lot that his idea of "home" was Bisbee, not his apartment in Tucson. "Only you, *querido*," she said. That got her another kiss. Miles waved goodbye and walked out to his car.

"What does *querido* mean? I've heard that before," Fiona said. "And what is *mi novio*? I heard you refer to Miles as *mi novio*."

"*Mi novio* is like my boyfriend, but more serious than a casual boyfriend. *Querido* means loved one, beloved, dear one, something like that. Miles get all squishy when I call him Spanish endearments."

"Squishy, huh?"

"I should add that all Miles has to do is look at me, and I get all squishy."

Both Fiona and Cat laughed.

"I guess I'll do some more exploring," Fiona said. "Is it okay if I take Greta again?"

"Sure. I'm going to go see Renata. I'll take Tito with me. See you later."

~~~

Renata's mother lived in the Warren district so Cat took her car and drove over. Tito sat in the back seat. She found Señora Romero's house quickly, as it was only a couple of blocks from the ball park.

"So this is where Miles comes for his cooking lessons," Cat said. Tito looked at her and wagged his tail.

Señora Romero answered Cat's knock. "Come in, Catalina. Renata is waiting for you. Señor Miles is not with you?"

"No, he's gone to Tucson. He'll be back tomorrow. How is Renata doing?"

"Better, I think. But she will need time to heal. They were rough with her."

Cat followed Señora Romero into her living room. Renata was sitting upright in a recliner chair. She smiled and waved when she saw Cat.

"Memo called me and told me you were coming," she said.

"How are you feeling?" To Cat, Renata looked quite pale.

"A lot better. My mom is making a fuss over me. Memo is, too. He's coming later to stay here. He thinks he's going to be my bodyguard." Renata smiled. "Isn't he sweet?"

"Well, every girl needs a bodyguard sometime in her life." Cat returned her smile. "Now it's your time. Actually, maybe you need more than one bodyguard."

"Memo said he has two friends from high school who can be here too, for a couple of nights anyway. Those dudes were both
~~~

on the high school wrestling team." She laughed. "Three body-guards!"

"That's good news."

"Have a seat." Renata turned to her mom. *"Mama, por favor, tráele un café."* Please bring her a coffee.

"Claro," her mom answered. Of course.

"Gracias," Cat said. Señora Romero disappeared into her kitchen.

"And there's that big boy, Tito. He's visited the Star so frequently that he's become popular with everyone, the regular customers and the staff, too." Renata reached out for Tito. He approached and got his ears rubbed. Then he turned and settled himself onto a rug.

Cat sat on the couch. "So how are you doing? I mean, really?"

"I was drugged, but I bet you know that."

Cat nodded. "Do the doctors know what kind of drug?"

"No. They took blood and urine samples. Chief Morales said they'll figure it out in a day or two."

"Your mom says they were rough on you. What did she mean?"

"These two guys came to my apartment. One was the white-suit guy who threw that woman off the hotel balcony into the street. The other was a tough guy, like an enforcer. He hit me a couple of times." She pushed back her hair and pointed to a bruise over her eye. "And after they drugged me, they must have just thrown my body around because I'm sore all over."

"No broken bones?"

"No. Just bruises."

Señora Romero returned with a cup of coffee for Cat. She returned to the kitchen.

"Do you feel like talking about what happened?"

"Yes. I'm so glad you're here, Cat. Chief Morales came by yesterday evening and I made a statement. But as the drugs wear off, my thinking gets clearer and I can remember more. I'd like to tell you some new things now."

"Sure. I want to help. But you may need to talk to Sam Morales again if you have additional information."

Renata nodded. "How much do you already know?"

"Brett Jamison came into the gallery with some of his art. He told me how you two saw each other early Friday morning. He said you had been jogging when you and Brett saw that woman come off the balcony. So I know about the man in the white suit."

"Yeah, that's right. There was a man up there above us. First, he threw off a big piece of pottery. Then he jerked that woman by her arm toward him, picked her up and threw her off, too." Renata drew back and shook her head. "It was really horrible. I've never seen anyone killed like that. Actually, I've never seen anyone killed at all. I hope I never do again." She looked at Cat. "Do you know who she is? Was, I mean."

"No. Sam said they haven't been able to identify her yet. Tell me about the man on the balcony."

"I'll admit I was looking more at the woman. But I remember he was fairly young, in his twenties, with dark hair. He looked like a Mexican. Kind of like me and my family. He had on this really nice ivory-colored suit. Dressy. Expensive. I think he had a gold chain around his neck."

"You decided to run?"

"Yes. He looked directly at me. He had this really scary-looking scowl on his face. When he turned to come down the stairs toward me, I took off. I don't think he ever saw Brett."

"No. We're kind of keeping it quiet that Brett was even there. So where did you go?"

"I ran back to my apartment above the Star Tavern. It was still early morning. I thought I'd lost him because when I looked back, I couldn't see him anywhere. I went upstairs to my apartment. Everything was quiet for about thirty minutes and then they came for me."

"They?"

"Yeah, the man in the white suit and another man. He was Mexican, too, but taller and beefier. I'm not sure how they got into the tavern. Probably the back door on the alley. They came up the stairs and smashed open my apartment door. The man in the white suit started trashing everything. He just picked up anything and everything and threw it. He made a total mess of my apartment. The big guy came for me right away. He started hitting me. He had this blank look on his face, like he was just doing his job." Renata shook her head no. "I tried to fight back, but I was no match for that guy."

"Did they say anything to you?"

"Almost nothing. The dude in the white suit said only one thing. When I screamed out, 'What do you want from me? Why are you doing this?' his answer was, 'You're in the way.'"

"In the way?" Cat shook her head. "It sounds like this is about more than seeing him kill that woman. He could have just run, got lost, left Bisbee immediately, I mean. Maybe he's got some plan in action here, he wants to stay here, and your ability to recognize him is a problem for him."

"I don't know, Cat. I can't tell you much more about this because the big guy held me down and the white-suit guy jabbed a needle in my arm. I passed out almost immediately."

"And that's all you remember?"

"No. I remember more now. That's why I'm glad you're here so I can tell you."

"I'm listening."

"They took me somewhere. I don't know where. I started to wake up, but I could hear people talking so I held still and didn't open my eyes. I was too scared. Then I heard two voices coming closer. There was a woman, and the second voice sounded like the white-suit man. The woman was really criticizing the man very harshly."

"What do you mean?"

"She dominated the conversation. She called him all sorts of insults: *tonto, imbécil, lerdo, estúpido.* Like he was a real dumbshit."

"Fool, imbecile, dumb, stupid. Wow. No holding back. So clearly she was in control."

"Yeah, and he was whining like a four-year-old. But he deferred to her."

"No idea who she is?"

"No. I've never seen her before. I opened my eyes just a squint. She's older than white-suit guy, maybe she's in her mid-forties, she was dressed nicely, she had longish dark hair, and she was clearly in control. At one point, she called him by his name, Mateo. She said, 'Mateo, this idea you have about Chinese art has to be one of the stupidest things you've ever come up with.'"

"Chinese art?" Cat felt a wave of concern come over her. She immediately thought of Ted Yang.

Renata nodded. "He argued with her in that whining voice, but I couldn't hear exactly what he was saying except that the word *dinero* kept coming up."

"Money," said Cat.

"Also, when she was berating him, she complained that he was screwing up some business project she was working on now. That's where the *dinero* came in. She said he was going to attract attention to what she was doing and cause her to lose money."

"No idea what her business project is?"

"No. And even worse, I think he was planning to kill me. She let him know in no uncertain terms that killing me would be a really bad idea. She said, 'So now you want a second body for us to have to deal with? Are you aware that you are attracting police attention? *Estúpido.*' I could hear the contempt in her voice."

"So she saved your life," Cat said.

Renata nodded.

They both became quiet. Finally, Renata looked at Cat and said, "That's all I remember because they jabbed me again with more of that drug. I didn't wake up again until I was found outside the tavern. Someone called an ambulance, and they took me to the hospital."

Cat stood. "Knowing this man's first name, Mateo, could come in helpful. And what you learned about this woman is very intriguing. I bet that will be important, too. For now, though, I think you need to call Sam Morales and ask him to come and visit again. He needs to know all this."

"Okay. I'll call him."

"I'm going to go now so you can rest. Come on, Tito." Cat and Tito headed for the door.

Renata nodded. "I'll let you know if I remember anything else."

Cat and Tito left the Romero house and headed home. On their way there, Cat thought again about the woman and two men sitting in the corner of the Star Tavern on Saturday night.

~~~

Cat drove up her street to her gallery. She noticed there was a car in front so she pulled in behind the gallery and parked. Tito accompanied her, walking at her side into the gallery's back door. She immediately went into the main room of the gallery. She could see a man standing at the front door. He was dressed in a white suit.

"Uh oh," Cat said in a low voice. "Tito, you're going to take care of me, right?"

Tito looked up at her and wagged his tail.

Cat unlocked the door. "Hi," she said to the man. "I'm sorry, but we're not open on Mondays. Could you come back tomorrow?"

The man slipped past her, and Cat found herself stepping backwards to avoid contact. The man walked directly into the gallery, and said, "I'm just visiting. I'm not sure I'll be in Bisbee tomorrow."

Cat noticed that he was young, probably mid-twenties, very handsome, Hispanic, with dark eyes and hair. Everything about him suggested a high level of confidence. He looked just like the description that both Renata and Brett Jamison had given her about the man in the white suit.
~~~

"My name is Cat Miranda." She couldn't help but notice that Tito had stepped in front of her. Now her dog was standing between her and the man. Cat knew that her dog had gone into protection mode. She trusted Tito's sense about this dude.

"Could I just take a quick look around?" It was obvious to Cat that he was going to get his way, regardless of what she said. "I'm curious about the kinds of art produced by local artists. I hear you have the best gallery in Bisbee."

"Well, I'm glad to hear that that I have a good reputation," Cat answered. She made note of the fact that he had not told her his name despite her self-introduction.

The man began a casual survey of the paintings on the wall. He stopped at the back of the gallery to look closely at a case with glass and pottery pieces. Then he continued looking at the paintings on the opposite wall.

"Very nice," he said as he looked at a landscape, one of the paintings brought in by Brett Jamison on the day before her exhibition.

"Jamison is a local artist." Cat couldn't help but wonder if this man knew that Brett had seen him and the dead woman.

"Do you sell art online?" The man turned and smiled at Cat. It was not a particularly friendly smile.

"I have a website for the gallery, and I feature different artists there. But I haven't had time to do any extensive marketing. Usually if someone orders a piece off the website, it's because they saw it first when they came into the gallery. I mean, for example, a tourist who was here in Bisbee and visited the gallery."

"So you're not one of those agents who find art for other websites or galleries or whatever?"

"No."

The man turned to Cat and looked directly at her. "Do you have any Chinese art?"

"Chinese?" she said. That was a surprise, and strange. She thought immediately of Ted Yang. She had a strong feeling that she should say nothing about Yang to this guy. And she remembered what Renata had told her about the mysterious woman's comments regarding Chinese art. If this guy wants Chinese art, Cat wasn't going to help him find it, not in Bisbee anyway.

"No. All the artists in my gallery are from Bisbee. Nothing Chinese. Are you looking for Chinese art?"

"Yes, I'm a collector."

"Oh, well, you may have to go somewhere else for that. West Coast probably, or Phoenix, maybe. I don't know anything about the Chinese art market. Sorry."

Cat thought that the man had a rather satisfied look on his face.

As they walked around the gallery, Tito made sure that he stayed in front of Cat, between her and the man in the white suit.

"Well, I'll be going now. Thanks so much for allowing me to look around."

Before Cat could say anything, the man in the white suit was out the front door of the gallery, heading for his car.

"That dude is trouble," Cat said to Tito, stroking is head. "I'm glad you're here, *mi chiquitito*. You're such a good boy." Tito wagged his tail and licked her hand. Cat locked up the gallery, and, together, they went to her house.

9 A Clue

The next morning, Cat and Fiona met in the kitchen again. Cat handed Fiona a cup of coffee. "What happened to your brother? I haven't seen him since…I don't know when."

"Trevor got a ride over to Sierra Vista. There's something there called the Ramsey Canyon Preserve. It's run by the Nature Conservancy. He talked to someone in the visitor center. She told him she would 'guaran-damn-tee' that Trevor would see hummingbirds if he came for a visit."

Cat chuckled. "That's true. They've made a point of attracting hummers, so he'll probably see a gazillion of them there, and he'll see several other bird species, too."

"Trevor took his camping gear with him. He may be gone a couple of days."

Cat nodded. "That's good. He'll enjoy it."

They were quiet for a few minutes then Fiona said, "Cat, do you think I could hang out with you today. I'm very curious about this murder, and I'd like to stay current. Maybe I could help."

"Sure," Cat said. "But you don't think you'll miss having Greta with you all day?"

Fiona grinned. "I think Greta and I can live without each other for a few hours. Probably that would be better because I'm concerned that we might get too attached to each other. But knowing her has made me think that I need to get a dog of my own when I go home. I miss having a dog companion."

"Won't that be difficult? Having a dog and traveling a lot?"

"Actually I'm thinking about a major lifestyle change. I'm seriously considering just staying at home and writing a book…or several books. I can still support myself with those business-related blogs I told you about. I have a long list of ideas for nonfiction books based on my travels. And I'm considering writing a novel, too."

"Really? What kind of novel? Literary or genre?"

"Genre. Science fiction or speculative fiction. I read in that genre a lot."

"I need to introduce you to Jake McKenna. He's the bouncer at Amanda's tavern. He just published his first sci-fi book."

"Oh, I'd really enjoy meeting him."

"Okay. I'll track him down. He wasn't at the Star Tavern on Saturday night. So unless you want more coffee, I suggest we go find Brett Jamison and see if he has any ideas on identifying the dead woman or that dude in the white suit. But first, I have to feed the dogs."

~~~

Almost an hour later, Cat and Fiona arrived at Brett's art studio.

"Welcome, ladies. Please come in." Brett greeted them at his door with a big grin on his face.

"I think you met Fiona at the art opening on Saturday," Cat said.

"Yes. Hi, Fiona. Good to see you again."

"And you." Fiona looked around the room. "You've created some really beautiful paintings, Brett. I like the abstract landscapes the best."

"Thank you. I love painting them."

"You seem especially cheerful, Brett. Did something good happen?" Cat asked.

"Yes! My beautiful girl Hannah has agreed to marry me, *and* she's going to start teaching here in Bisbee in January. They found a replacement for her at her school in Tucson, and at the same
~~~

time, a new job opened up for her here in Bisbee. We'll get to live together, too. Everything just came together perfectly for us."

"Congratulations, Brett. I'm happy for you."

"You'll get an invitation to the wedding, Cat, and you, too, Fiona, if you're still here."

"Brett, we're actually here for a far less cheerful task," Cat said. "We're trying to find out as much as possible about the dead woman you saw. As you know, Renata Romero was abducted. She's back home now, but I'm concerned about all this violence we're experiencing. The more we know, the better off we'll be."

"I think I told you everything I know." Brett had a serious look on his face. "I showed you the photos, didn't I?"

"No! You have photos?"

"Gosh, I'm such a space case." He reached over to a table nearby and found his smart phone. He looked at it for a minute then handed it to Cat. "Sorry. This is unpleasant. We're looking at a dead body here."

Cat took the phone and stared at it. Fiona peered over Cat's shoulder. They both reacted to the photo of the dead woman with frowns and expressions of dismay.

"It's kind of hard to see her face," Cat finally said. "It's sort of sideways against the pavement."

"Yeah. That's how she landed." Brett's smile had disappeared.

"Looks to me like she may be a middle-aged Caucasian woman," Fiona said. "Graying hair, a bit on the plump side."

"I agree," Cat said. "And you've never seen her before?"

"No," Brett said. "I'm certain that she's never been in my studio. I don't think she's a local either. She must be a tourist. I don't have any idea why this guy threw her off the balcony. Sorry to say I didn't get a very good look at his face or a photo of him."

"What's this?" Cat asked, looking intently at Brett's phone.

"That's a photo I took of the broken pot that he threw off the balcony. I don't know why I took that photo."

"That pot, even smashed up, looks familiar. Maybe it's a clue that will help us figure out what's going on," she said. "Could you please send this photo to my smart phone?"

"Sure."

Cat received the photo very quickly. "Okay, Brett, we've taken enough of your time. If you think of anything or remember anything else, let me know. And be sure to let us know when the wedding will be held. I'll come prepared to dance."

Brett grinned. "You bet."

~~~

"Okay, Fiona. Let's go to Michael and Willow Dimaio's ceramics studio," Cat said.

"Yes, I remember meeting them at your art opening," Fiona replied.

Michael had just unlocked the entrance door to the shop and turned the "Closed" sign around to "Open" when they arrived. "Come on in," he said to Cat and Fiona. He called out to Willow, "Is the coffee ready yet?"

Willow stuck her head out of a back room and waved. "Coming!"

Five minutes later, all four were sitting around a small table. Willow had placed a tray with four cups of coffee on the table. Everyone took a cup.

"Thanks for seeing us," Cat said. "I'm hoping to find out more about the woman who was killed. I'm worried about Renata. You know about her abduction?"

Willow and Michael both nodded.

"And you know that Brett Jamison saw the whole thing?"

"We heard a rumor," Willow said. Michael nodded.

"We just came from Brett's studio. It turns out he had taken a couple of photos that morning. Let me show you."

"Oh my god," Willow gasped when she saw the dead woman's body. Michael shook his head and frowned.
~~~

"Do you think you know this woman?" Cat asked.

Michael cocked his head. "It's hard to see her, but she kind of looks like a tourist who came in a few days ago. She looked at everything in the shop."

"I know who Michael is talking about. That woman didn't buy anything," Willow added.

Cat turned to the next photo of the broken pot.

"Hey!" Michael said. "That looks like our pot. That's the one that was stolen. What the hell?"

Willow took the phone in her hand and looked closely. "Yes, this is one of the pots from our Native American collection. It's from Jemez Pueblo in New Mexico. I'm pretty sure that this is the pot that was stolen. The colors are unique."

"You mentioned you might be able to get a look at a neighbor's security video."

"Yes, I checked with the neighbor and looked at the video. There was nothing of interest on it."

"This photo of the broken pot could be very useful when making an insurance claim," Fiona said.

"Oh, yes!" Michael responded. "Great idea! I'll follow up on that for sure."

Cat stood up. "I'll ask Brett to send you the photo of the pot since it's his to share. We'll be going now. Thanks so much for all the information. Very useful."

"And thanks for the coffee," Fiona added.

Back out on the street, Fiona asked Cat, "Where do we go now?"

"I think we should check in with Ana Hernandez."

~~~

Cat and Fiona found Ana in her office, sitting behind her desk, her gaze alternating between her computer monitor and a pile of papers. She stood, welcomed them, and invited them to sit.

"Need anything to drink? Coffee? Water?"
~~~

"No, thanks. We just had a coffee," Cat said.

"Are you here to catch me up on everything?" Ana asked, smiling.

Fiona noticed that Ana looked very much like a lawyer today. She was dressed in a dark, tailored suit with an ivory-colored blouse and small gold earrings, not the casual slacks and sweater she wore when she came to dinner at Cat's house and flirted with Fiona's brother.

"Yes, exactly." Cat gave Ana a summary of her conversations with Renata, Brett, and also, Michael and Willow Dimaio. She also showed Ana the photos Brett had taken of the dead woman's body and of the broken pot. She went into detail on exactly what Renata had told her. And she told them both about the visit of the white-suited man to her gallery who wanted to know if she sold Chinese art.

"Hmmm…" Ana looked closely at the photos. "Interesting. And Sam Morales hasn't been able to identify this woman?"

"Sam told me that she had no identification on her at all, and they haven't found a purse. He hasn't been able to find any record of her staying at a local hotel either, but not knowing her name has made that even more difficult. His staff is searching missing persons databases now. That's not easy because they don't have a photo of her. They don't even know about this one Brett took, although it's not all that helpful anyway."

"Any results from an autopsy? She may have already been dead by the time she hit the pavement."

"I don't know about any autopsy. I didn't ask him about that," Cat said.

"She probably had no identification on her because the killer took it," Ana said. "The woman's credit card info might turn out to be useful, though. Any business in Bisbee that took her credit card should have her personal name, or the name of her business. The next task would be to find someone who could match the photo with the name on the credit card. That could take a lot of time."

"Yes, that makes sense," Cat said. "Maybe we'll get lucky."

"What Renata overheard could turn out to be very useful," Ana responded. "Those comments are pretty damning. Based on what Renata heard the mystery woman say, it seems quite likely that white-suit man murdered this woman. What did you say his name is? Mateo? But we don't know why he murdered the woman. What is his interest in Chinese art? Does the dead woman have anything to do with Chinese art? We don't know. The mystery woman who was berating the white-suit man was very disdainful about his Chinese art thing, but she seemed mainly concerned that his antics would draw attention to whatever she's doing. And what would that be?"

"Probably something illegal," Cat said.

Fiona was grinning now. "You two are plotting a great mystery-suspense novel."

"The problem is that we don't know who did what. So our plot is full of holes now," Cat said.

Ana chuckled. "Cat, I have confidence in you. I think you are very good at filling in holes."

"So we don't know enough right now," Cat said. "Ana, are you ready for a lunch break? I suggest we all go to Jillie's to eat. Then Fiona can try out more of our Sonoran cuisine."

"Excellent idea," Ana said. She looked at her watch. "Sure. Let me save everything here on my computer and then I'll go with you."

~~~

Ana's office was quite close to Jillie's café in downtown Bisbee. They arrived before the noon rush hour, and they quickly ordered. As predicted, Fiona had several Sonoran cuisine options to choose from. This time, though, the dishes were all vegan. After all, Jillie's café specialized in vegan dishes.

The three had almost finished their meal when Jillie appeared. Cat introduced Fiona and invited Jillie to sit with them. Fiona
~~~

made note of Jillie's appearance: late thirties or maybe forty years old, slender, dark hair knotted behind her head and a chef's hat, too. She wore dark-rimmed glasses, and she would have looked really serious except for the grin on her face.

"How's it going, Jillie?" Cat asked.

"Great! I mean 'great' if the goal is to have lots of business. Our reputation as an excellent place to eat is growing, and we always have a crowd here, both at lunch and dinner. But if the goal is for me to have some free time, then not so great. I'm seriously considering hiring more staff so I can get a day off every now and then." Jillie chuckled. "I'm not complaining though."

"We all need a little rest," Cat responded. "Jillie, while we're here, I'm hoping you might be able to help us with a problem."

"Yes," Ana added. "We're trying to identify someone. We're hoping she may have eaten here. If not, we're going to have to contact many of the businesses in Bisbee to see if anyone knows her."

"Who are you trying to identify?" Jillie asked.

"You heard about the woman who was thrown off the East-West Hotel balcony and ended up dead on Tombstone Canyon Road?" Cat asked.

"Yes, everyone is talking about that. Terrible business."

"We have a photo of her." Cat pulled her smart phone out. "Sorry, but it's her dead in the street."

Jillie looked at the phone and frowned. "Gosh. That's awful." She stared at the photo. "I don't know her name. But I do recognize her. Or at least I think I recognize her. She ate here a couple of times last week."

"Any chance she may have used a credit card?" Ana asked. "You might be able to access her name from that transaction. We're trying to identify her by name."

"That's possible," Jillie answered. "Many of my customers do use credit cards to pay for their meals. How about if I send out some ice cream for you all while I go to my office in the back and see if I can find her?"

They all smiled and nodded.

"Brilliant," said Fiona. "I love ice cream."

Jillie disappeared, and one of her wait staff brought the ice cream.

"Yummy," Cat said.

"What is this?" Fiona asked.

"Yours is *almendra*. That's almond," Ana said. "I have *choco menta*…chocolate mint, and Cat's is *piña*…I mean pineapple. Sometime you should try *aguacate* which is avocado. That sounds weird, but it makes really good *helado*."

They had just finished eating their ice cream when Jillie reappeared.

"I found her," Jillie said, waving a piece of paper. "She used a business credit card. Her name is Sylvia Chen and the business is Chen Associates. There's nothing that tells you what Chen Associates does for a business. Just her name. Here, I wrote it down for you."

Cat took the paper and said, "Thanks so much, Jillie. You've saved us a lot of time and work. I'll be sure to let our police chief Sam Morales know about this."

"I have to get back to work," Ana said. "Thanks for the great meal. You're the best, Jillie."

"So nice to meet you," Fiona added. "I'm a travel writer for several British and European publications, and I often write about food and restaurants. If you don't mind, I'd like to write about your restaurant. Five star review, of course."

"Wonderful!" Jillie clapped her hands. "I would love having some guests from England or any of those other places. Europe, I mean. Yes. Totally cool!"

Fiona nodded. "Consider it done. I took a couple of photos, too, to go with the article."

Suddenly the sound of sirens came drifting into the restaurant.

"I wonder what's going on now," Cat said.

"Sounds like a fire truck," Ana said.

"Thanks again, Jillie," Cat and Fiona said at once. They both stood.

As they left the restaurant, Cat said to Ana. "Chen? That's a Chinese name."

"This woman does not look Asian. She's Caucasian. Chen may be her married name," Ana said. "This is a start. Okay. I'm off. If you need me, I'll be back at my office."

"Later, when I have time, I'll ask Google about Chen Associates," Cat added. She waved goodbye to Ana and then turned to Fiona. "We're very close to a new gallery going in. The gallerist is Ted Yang, and yes, he's Chinese, or more accurately, Chinese American. I'm doing graphic design for him, and I've already started his website. Want to go take a look at the new gallery? It's not ready yet but you'll get an idea."

"Yes, please."

They walked a block deeper into downtown Bisbee then turned on a side street. Much to their surprise, there was both a firetruck and an ambulance in the side street. A small crowd had gathered.

"Oh my god," Cat said. "That's Ted's new place." She turned to look at the bystanders. She immediately spotted Jessica Weber, one of the librarians at Bisbee's Copper Queen Library. She was Ted's girlfriend. Cat approached Jessica.

"Hi, Jessica. What happened?"

Jessica Weber was wiping away tears and struggling to not start sobbing again. "I was at work. We heard the sirens, and I realized they'd stopped at Ted's place so I came to see. Some guys went in there when Ted was working on the place. They beat him up and then threw some kind of incendiary device into the gallery."

"How is Ted?" Cat looked at Jessica, her slender build, straight black hair, and her face and eyes. She didn't really look totally Chinese but she didn't look totally Caucasian either. Mixed race, for sure. She could pass as Navajo if she weren't so fair. Interesting how the genes mix and create something new.

"Ted talked to me as they were putting him in the ambulance. He said he's pretty sure he'll be okay, but he agreed to go to the hospital to be checked out. He said there were two of them. They didn't say anything. They just went for him and beat him up. He has no idea why. I'm taking off work early, and I'm going to the hospital to be with him. I'll stay with him tonight and for as long as he needs me." She stifled a sob.

"And the fire?"

"It did a lot of damage. I don't know much about that. The fire is out now."

Cat could see Chief of Police Sam Morales and his new deputy Dave Chapman interviewing people.

"If you need anything, call me," Cat said. She reached out and squeezed Jessica's hand. Jessica nodded and moved away.

Cat shook her head as she and Fiona watched the ambulance drive away with Ted Yang. "Whew, this has been a crazy, crazy day."

"Yes," Fiona, "crazy, but very interesting."

"I'll check on Ted tomorrow. Let's go home. I want to be there when Miles gets back from Tucson."

"Time to get squishy, huh?"

"Priorities. Priorities." Cat grinned. "Squishy comes first."

Fiona laughed.

The two women headed west on Tombstone Canyon Road away from downtown Bisbee. They were back at Cat's house fifteen minutes later.

10 Captivity

Fiona met Cat and Miles in the kitchen early on Wednesday morning.

"I'll take just a half a cup of coffee. I'm meeting Luca for breakfast," Fiona said.

"Oh, that's nice," said Cat. "Where's he taking you?"

"I don't know. He said he has a surprise for me." Fiona gulped down the coffee. She stood and adjusted her backpack. "Luca told me to bring some water, so I'm wearing my backpack today so I can carry my thermos." She retrieved her phone from her pants pocket and deposited it into a hidden compartment in the backpack.

"Water is always a good idea," Cat said.

Fiona drank her coffee quickly. "I'll see you later." She waved goodbye and headed out the door, walking toward downtown Bisbee.

"And you, Sir Miles," Cat giggled. "What are you going to do today?"

"You just can't help yourself, can you?" Miles grinned. "Call me 'sir' and you laugh."

"Oh, Sir Miles, you are such a hottie." Cat batted her eyelashes.

"What? No laugh? Hottie? Want to go back to bed?"

"I wish," Cat said, "but I have work to do. I'm going to check on Ted Yang today, and also try to figure out who Sylvia Chen is. There's a mystery here and I want to know more. Maybe we can meet in bed later."

"We can. I'm available."

"And nice things will happen?"

"Of course. Meanwhile, I'm free on mid-winter vacation now. I'm thinking about reading a book."

"Reading a book? Why am I not surprised? You are such a book nerd."

"But first, I'm taking these dogs for a run."

"Good. Please try to wear Greta out and maybe she'll manage to not destroy anything."

Miles hugged and kissed her. "Okay. I'm off." He called the dogs. They responded quickly, tails wagging.

~~~

Fiona was only about a block away from Cat's house when she saw Luca coming down a side street toward her. He had a back-pack on his back, too, and a big smile on his face.

"Hi, Luca. So where are we going?"

"Hello, sweet Fiona. See that street up ahead? We'll go up that street, find a trail about halfway up the hill, and we'll follow the trail to a special spot."

"Why is it special?"

"We can sit in the sun if it's cold and sit under the shade of a big mesquite tree if it's hot. But the real reason that it's special to me is because I will be there with you."

Fiona smiled. "Sounds like fun. You brought something to eat?"

"I did. You won't go hungry. I have *tortas de huevos con queso. Y fruta.*"

"*Fruta* is fruit. That's all I know. I thought I knew some Span-ish, but I have come to realize I know next to nothing."

"Mexican sandwiches with eggs and cheese. Don't worry. I'll teach you." He grinned.

At that moment, they both turned toward the sound of a ve-hicle coming toward them at a rapid speed. A black BMW was
~~~

barreling up Tombstone Canyon Road from downtown Bisbee. Before Fiona and Luca could react, the BMW came to an abrupt halt next to them. A man in a dark suit jumped out of the passenger seat. He pointed a gun at them and growled, "*Entra en el coche.*"

"He wants us to get in the car," Luca said.

"We'd better do what he says. He has a gun."

The man held the gun on them until they were both seated in the backseat. The driver didn't bother even looking at them. The car did a turnaround in the middle of the street and headed east.

Fiona took Luca's hand. She was scared. He squeezed her hand.

Ten minutes later, Fiona realized that they had left Old Bisbee and now were in the Warren district. The car was going at a steady speed, but not fast enough to attract the attention of any cops who might be nearby. The BMW made a couple of turns on to narrower streets and stopped in front of a house painted a sage green color. Fiona could see the numbers 1403 over the front door, which was up a short flight of stairs from street level.

The two men exited the front seat of the car and opened the back doors.

"*Sal!*" one of the men said roughly. "*Andele!*"

"I bet that means 'get out,'" Fiona said.

Luca nodded. They both got out of the back seat. One of the men gestured toward an open garage door on the lower level of the house. This was one of those houses Fiona had noticed earlier. The home was upstairs and, in this case, the lower level was a garage. One of the men opened the garage door then the two men pushed Fiona and Luca into the garage. The men in dark suits stripped them of their backpacks. Each man took a backpack, zipped open the backpack compartments, and dumped everything onto the garage floor. Luca's backpack had sandwiches, juice containers, cups, napkins, and Luca's cell phone. Fiona's backpack only had her water thermos, a small notebook and a pen. Her cell phone stayed in its secret compartment.

One of the men pocketed Luca's phone, and the other grabbed Fiona's notebook.

"Hey!" said Fiona. "Leave that alone."

The man holding the notebook reached out and slapped her hard in the face.

Luca jumped forward and punched the man's jaw. At that, both men attacked Luca, punched him repeatedly, knocked him down, and smashed his face against the rough concrete floor. They turned, opened the garage door, exited and closed the door behind them. Fiona could hear them lock the door. They had taken her notebook with them.

She went to Luca. "Oh, Luca. How bad is it?"

"Just roughed up. I'll be okay."

She retrieved a tissue from her pocket and wiped blood away from a cut above his eye. "I think you may end up with a black eye. And your cheek and jaw are bruised."

"What's in that notebook? Anything you want to keep secret, like passwords or whatever?"

"No. Nothing like that. It's mostly a list of Spanish words with their translation into English. I have another notebook for my reporting, but I didn't bring it today."

Luca nodded.

"I'll try to get help." She reached for her backpack, opened the secret compartment, retrieved her smart phone, and sent a series of texts to Cat.

Abducted by two men. With Luca. Taken to Warren. House number 1403. Street? Close to ballpark. Help!

"I've texted Cat and asked her to come and rescue us."

Luca looked at her phone and then at Fiona.

"You are very clever to hide your phone like that."

"I've traveled a lot and I've learned the hard way. I'd say I'm more experienced than I am clever."

Fiona tried to call 911, too, but her phone had gone dead, and the call didn't go through. She turned to Luca and shrugged her shoulders. "I don't know what the problem is with my phone. There's no connection now. I hope my texts got through to Cat."

Luca smiled. "Want to eat something while we wait?"

"Good idea."

Luca retrieved the sandwiches, still in a plastic bag. "Here's some orange juice, too." He handed her a bottle.

"Yum…this is good," Fiona said.

"Thank you. I made the *tortas*."

After they ate, they explored the garage and looked for a way into the home above. They found what appeared to be a door that likely led to stairs and the upper level, but the door was nailed shut.

An hour passed. They said little to each other. Luca went to sit on a pile of burlap seed bags against an inner wall.

"Why do you suppose Cat hasn't answered you?"

"She told me once that she often turns off her smart phone so she won't be interrupted. That may be what's going on now."

They became quiet again.

Fiona broke the silence. "It's sunny outside." She was standing on her tiptoes peering out of the narrow slit of window high in the basement wall. The window was much too small for her to exit through it. She sighed.

"Not like England this time of year, is it?"

Fiona turned to look at him. He was still sitting on the pile of burlap bags.

"No. This time of year it's often rainy and cold in England. And it snows sometimes."

"Do you like it here?"

"Yes, Bisbee is a lovely little town, and I like all the people I've met. Cat is a real sweetheart, and I love her dogs, especially Greta. But I'll admit. I'm a little homesick."

"Really? Why?"

Fiona came and sat beside Luca. His cheek was turning from irritated red to a bruised blue. The cut over his eye looked puffy and red. Even so, he was so handsome. Those soft dark curls that almost touched his shoulders, and those deep, dark brown eyes. She knew he was trying to distract her, to get her to think about something other than being held prisoner in this strange place. She frowned. She had really conflicting feelings about him. She had decided already that she was going to say good-bye to Luca Sutherland. She was going to leave him behind, leave behind all this craziness, and go home. If, that is, they could figure out a way out of here. She sighed. At the same time, she really, really liked Luca, and she really wanted to help him out of whatever mess he was in. Yes, she really liked him a lot.

"I've had a good trip," she said. "I really enjoyed seeing every place I visited and doing everything I did. Mexico City surprised me. I'm not sure what I was expecting. But it turned out to be a very beautiful city, very sophisticated with lots of art galleries and fabulous restaurants. And for history buffs, Mexico City is a great place to visit. It was originally the home of the Aztec empire. But I bet you know that already. And the U.S. is…" she paused, "…a beautiful country, too, especially the American West. I've already written and published several travel articles about both Mexico City and destinations in the Southwest states, Arizona and New Mexico, in particular. And I have material for even more articles." She paused. "But some of the people I've met drive me crazy sometimes."

Luca chuckled. "And why is that?"

"Well," Fiona looked directly at him. "Some of them seem to be very open, but in reality, there are things they keep hidden. Things they don't tell you." She stared into Luca's eyes until he looked away.

"You're talking about me, aren't you?" He was frowning now.

"Yes. I think you know a whole lot more than you're telling me."

Luca fell silent and stayed that way for several minutes. Fiona decided not to say anything. Maybe her silence would encourage him to open up.

"Yeah, you're right." Luca looked at her. "I was hoping to protect you from all this. I want more than anything for you to be safe."

Fiona nodded. "And?"

"And I don't want you think I'm a total, absolute fool."

Fiona smiled. "I bet this has something to do with a woman."

Luca's eyebrows went up in surprise. "How did you know?"

"Look. I have two little brothers. I saw them turn into fools once they reached puberty. All that testosterone made them crazy for a few years. They are better now that they are older. They actually think with their brains sometimes, not just with their knobs."

Luca nodded, smiling. "Yes. You just described me. Thinking with my knob."

"Who is she?"

"Was, not is. She's dead now." He looked down, frowning. "Everyone is dead."

"Okay. So there's a story, and I want to hear it. Start from the beginning."

Luca nodded. "Okay." He sighed deeply. "We had just returned to the U.S."

"We?"

"My family. My dad and my mom and me."

"Returned from where? Mexico?"

"No. England."

"*What*? England? What were you doing in England?"

"My dad worked there for an American company. We lived in London for several years. I did my A levels there."

Fiona laughed. "Maybe I'm the fool here. I never even considered you might have lived in the U.K." She waited. "Okay. I want to hear more. I want to know everything about you."

Luca reached out and took her hand. "You're so smart, Fiona. And so beautiful. And really so very sweet. I really, really like you. Please don't think I'm a total loser."

"I won't. You play the violin too well to be a total loser. I don't know why you think I'm sweet. Most people think I'm a hard arse."

"No. Not a hard ass. You can't fool me. I see the real you. Your true nature is to be gentle and sweet and loving. And very, very lovable."

Fiona felt intense embarrassment. She didn't know what to say.

Luca nodded and said, "Okay. Here goes. My dad was an American, and I was born in the U.S., but my mom is a Mexican citizen. So I have dual citizenship, American and Mexican. I have passports from both countries. When I was a kid, we lived in southern California, and we visited Mexico frequently. But then my dad was sent to England for his job. I lived there from age ten to almost eighteen."

Fiona shook her head. "I'm kind of shocked that you lived in England. Tell me more."

"That's why when I heard you speak for the first time, your English accent, I felt this kind of homesickness. It was surprising to realize that I felt that way. I didn't know I missed the U.K. so much. Of course, those years were peaceful, not like now. Anyway, after we lived in England for several years, my dad's company called him back, but right after we returned to the U.S., my dad had a heart attack and died."

"I'm sorry, Luca. That's so sad."

"My mom was really distraught. My dad wasn't that old, and his sudden death was a shock to both of us. My mom's family lives in Mexico. Her mother, *mi abuela*, that means 'grandmother' in Spanish, was still alive. So my mom decided for us to go live in Mexico to be close to her family. My mom was originally from Cuernavaca so that's where we went."

"I understand. That makes sense."

"Cuernavaca is a not far south of Mexico City. By that time, I was eighteen and it was time for me to go to university. So I enrolled in UNAM. That's Universidad Nacional Autónoma de

Mexico or National Autonomous University of Mexico. Do you understand my Spanish?"

"Only a little bit. Like I told you, I don't know much at all. I visited the UNAM campus. It's beautiful."

"The campus is on the south side of Mexico City so it wasn't too far from Cuernavaca. I could go visit my mom and keep an eye on her and *mi abuela* and all the other family members. I'm the last man in the family. No uncles."

"So you were how old then? And you were trying to take care of your family while you went to university?"

"Eighteen then. Yes. I was the only man in the family."

"What did you study?"

"Music. I went there for four years, and I earned my degree. I was talking with my mom about applying for a graduate program to get a master's degree. Either Julliard in New York City or the Royal College of Music in London."

"You thought about returning to England?"

"Yes, I liked the idea of returning. But I was concerned about leaving my mom and *mi abuela* in Mexico." He sighed deeply. "Then Mom and *mi abuela* were killed in a car wreck. A big truck smashed into them on the highway between Cuernavaca and Mexico City. They both died instantly."

"Oh, I'm so sorry."

"And then I did something really, really stupid."

"And this is where all the testosterone comes in?"

"Yes, it was partly testosterone and partly grief. I was looking for something or someone to help me deal with the pain of losing my family. But really, I don't know how I could have been so stupid. My rational mind was telling me that it was a huge mistake to get involved with Camila. But she was beautiful and sexy, and she came on to me. She wouldn't take no for an answer."

"What do you mean?"

"She invited me to her hotel room. I was playing with a musical group at a resort on the Caribbean coast, and she was there as a tourist. She invited me to her room and she grabbed me and started kissing me and taking off her clothes and taking off my clothes and the next thing I knew, we were in bed together naked and…" Luca shook his head. "We became lovers. We both returned to la Ciudad de Mexico, but separately. We secretly continued to see each other. Most of the times that we were together, we were in bed."

"So what's stupid about having a lover? Having a lover can be comforting."

"Camila told me from the first day that we had to keep our relationship a secret. She told me that her father was very strict and would not approve of her relationship with a younger man who was a musician. She even showed me a photo of her with her dad. He was an older guy in his fifties."

"You were about twenty-two? How old was she?"

"Yes. Twenty-two and she was twenty-eight. And the thing about being a musician is that she said her father would worry that I would never make enough money to take care of her. I had already figured out that she came from money. She had expensive jewelry and clothing and she was staying at a very expensive resort hotel when we first met."

"Her plan to was to introduce you to her dad slowly and hope that he'd come to like and respect you."

Luca looked at her. "You're so sweet. You always think of the best thing that could happen. No, it wasn't like that. It was worse than that. Far worse."

"So how was it?"

"Turns out that her dad was really her husband."

"Oh, no."

"Yeah. To top it off, her husband was a jefe in one of the biggest cartels in Mexico. La Familia Tamaulipas."

"So you were screwing the wife of a cartel boss?" Fiona shook her head. "Yeah, that's bad."

"Not *screwing*." Luca frowned. "I really cared about her. She finally told me the truth. She tried to get me to leave so I'd be safe, but I was too much in love with her. I convinced her to continue seeing me. So we agreed to be very, very careful and hope that he would never find out."

"Tamaulipas is over on the east side of Mexico, right?"

"Northeast. It's the Mexican state just south of the Texas Rio Grande border region."

"So what happened?"

"I asked her more than once if she wanted to leave him, but she told me that leaving just wasn't possible. He would know for sure that something wasn't right. He would know that he'd been cheated on."

"And her husband found out anyway?"

"Yeah. Camila called me one night. It's been well over a year ago now. She was crying, almost hysterical. She said her husband found out about us. She told me to run because he told her that he was going to find me and kill me. I believed her. I asked her to go with me. She said that wasn't possible."

"What happened to her?"

"She told me that she thought he would just beat her like he did the last time, and then let her go. She said that it was me he wanted to see dead. She begged me to disappear so he couldn't find me. And she promised to join me later. So I disappeared."

Like he did the last time? Fiona wondered what that meant. "Did you ever hear from her again?" she asked.

Luca shook his head. "I stayed in touch with some friends in Mexico City. Just three days after I went on the run, one of my friends told me that Camila had been murdered. Executed, really. She'd been shot in the head, and her body had been dumped in the middle of Paseo de la Reforma."

"Blimey. That's really bad. Paseo de la Reform is one of the major boulevards in Mexico City, right?"

"Yeah. Her body was dumped near the Angel. That's the Angel of Independence statue."

"Yes, I saw the Angel. It's famous."

"Clearly, he wanted the world to know that he wouldn't tolerate her infidelity. Then, just a couple of days after Camila's body was found, he died, too. Apparently he had a heart attack, maybe from the stress of all this. His name was Jorge Salazar."

They both fell silent. Fiona was trying to integrate a lot of information that was far more disturbing that she'd ever imagined.

"How did you end up in Bisbee?" she asked.

"I thought I'd be safer if I left Mexico and went north to the U.S. I avoided Texas because I thought it would be easier for them to find me there. So I went to the northwest, and I crossed the border at Nogales, Sonora, into Nogales, Arizona. That's when I saw an article about Bisbee, how it was an arts center and all that. I thought if I came here, I might get some gigs playing music. And some part-time work, too. No one would know me here. I thought maybe I'd be safe for a while until I could earn some money. My plan was to go farther north to a safer place and hope they'd never find me. But I stayed here too long. I like Bisbee."

"How old are you now anyway?" Fiona asked.

"I'm twenty-four. I'll be twenty-five in January." He paused for a moment. "How old are you?"

"Twenty-nine. I'll be thirty next April."

"I like older women." Luca grinned.

Fiona couldn't help it. She laughed. "But older women get you in trouble."

"Are you going to get me in trouble?"

Fiona shook her head. "You are such a flirt. Yes, I'll get you in trouble, but only good trouble."

"I could use some good trouble." His smile quickly faded. "So now you know what I mean about how I'm nothing but trouble. I'm the one more likely to get *you* in trouble and it will definitely be bad."

"What do you mean?"

"Jorge Salazar had a younger sister. Her name is Victoria. When Jorge died, word got around that Victoria held me responsible for her brother's death. She wants to see me dead. About the time I crossed the border, I got a message from a friend saying that Victoria was looking for me. It's likely that she'll deal with me in the same way her brother dealt with Camila. Shoot me in the head then dump my body on Paseo de la Reforma."

Fiona groaned and shook her head.

Luca sighed. "Recently I'd been thinking that maybe it was time for me to move on because I figured that eventually she would find me here. But I waited too long. I like it here, but I should have left much sooner."

"What does Victoria look like?"

"Mid-forties, longish dark hair, slender, always well-dressed, expensive jewelry, and she would be considered pretty if she didn't scowl all the time."

"I think I saw her."

"What? You saw Victoria Salazar?"

"When we went to the Star Tavern after the art opening, there was a woman sitting in a dark corner with two blokes. They looked like bodyguards. Cat noticed her, too. The woman was watching you."

"*Mierda*." He shook his head. "I should have left here months ago. I'm a fool. I'm so sorry to get you mixed up in this."

They fell silent again for a while.

"You could kiss me," Fiona said. She glanced sideways at him.

"Yes, I could." Luca was smiling again.

"But will you?"

"I will." Luca pulled her closer and began kissing her, gently at first, and then with more passion. Finally, he let her go. He was still smiling.

Fiona became aware that her heart was beating really fast. She had made a decision. She was scared, but she knew she'd made the right decision.

"Luca?"

"Yes?"

"We are leaving Bisbee as soon as we can get out of here, and you're going home with me."

"Home?"

"Yes, we're going home to England."

"Home? With you? I'd like that." His voice was soft.

She nodded. "Yes, we're going home. Together."

Fiona looked at Luca. His eyes were glistening. Luca took her hand in his, and they both leaned back against the wall.

Home. Yes. But first they had to get out of there, Fiona told herself. Where the hell was Cat Miranda?

11 Rescue, Departure

While Miles was running with the dogs, Cat went up to her office after Fiona left, and she began the search for Chen Associates. It didn't take her long to find several links to the company's website as well as some ads. She could see that it was not a large company, despite the active marketing efforts.

Chen Associates was based in Petaluma, California, not far north of San Francisco. The homepage, and nearly everything else on the website, had a link to a replica page that was in Chinese characters. She wondered if Ted Yang was planning on doing the same for his website. If so, he would have to do the translations. Cat didn't know a single word of Chinese, spoken or written.

Under the "About Us" tab, she learned that Chen Associates was involved in the business of acquiring "treasures" and making them available for resale to the Chinese market. There was a short list of employees. Mr. Vincent Chen was the CEO. Mrs. Sylvia Chen was listed as Chief Acquisitions Officer, and also as Mr. Chen's wife. There were two more employees, both with Hispanic surnames. One was a young woman at a desk who appeared to be the office secretary. The other was a young man in work clothes who probably did all the physical work, such as packing up "treasures" for shipment to buyers. Chen Associates was a small company.

What were the "treasures"? Cat wanted to know. There were links to pages with photos of either art or fine crafts. They fell into two categories: First were Chinese items that originated in

China but had ended up in America. Mostly these were older, either nineteenth or early twentieth century creations. This was the kind of thing Ted had told her about. The second category of treasures was all North American Indian arts and fine crafts.

Interesting, Cat thought. So these people were more-or-less in the same business as Ted Yang's planned project. Ted probably knew that he had competition, but he clearly felt he had advantages. He had really good contacts in China and his fluency in the language and culture were in his favor. And he was young, so he had time to build a business.

The other big difference was that the Chen business was acquiring and selling Native American arts and crafts, but Ted Yang had no plans to do that as far as Cat knew. And Sylvia Chen had stolen that pot from Michael and Willow. Clearly, ethics were not at the top of the list for Chen Associates.

Cat frowned. What does all this have to do with that dude Mateo, the one that Renata had encountered? Cat went over the brief conversation she'd had with him in her gallery. He clearly was interested in Chinese art. He'd asked her about Chinese art, and he'd asked her if she was an agent who finds art for others. She had to conclude that he was trying to find out if she was involved with Yang or if any other gallerists in town were involved in selling Chinese art, and possibly selling that Chinese art primarily to Chinese collectors.

What the hell, she thought to herself. Mateo is a Mexican dude. Why not Mexican art? Why Chinese? Does he actually know anything about Chinese art? She remembered what Renata had overheard. The mystery woman had said, "Mateo, this idea you have about Chinese art has to be one of the stupidest things you've ever come up with." So whoever she was, the mystery woman was not impressed with whatever Mateo was doing.

Cat was grateful that Mateo apparently believed her when she told him that she was not involved in anything having to do with Chinese art. So he'd left her alone after their brief encounter. What about other galleries in Bisbee? Had any of the gallerists been approached by him? And was he responsible for the attack on Ted Yang and his new gallery? After all, Ted had been quite open about his business plans.

If she could find other gallery owners who had been approached by Mateo, then she would know for sure that Mateo was trying to find potential competitors. And then eliminate them.

Time to call and see how Ted Yang was doing. She had his cell phone number, but when she called, his girlfriend Jessica Weber answered. Jessica told her that Ted had been seen in the hospital Emergency Room, and then he was sent home. His injuries weren't bad enough to admit him to the hospital.

"I'm taking care of him," Jessica said firmly. "He's taking a nap right now."

"That's good news that he has you there. He's really crazy about you, you know?" Cat said.

"The feeling is entirely mutual. I'm so in love with Ted."

"Did Ted tell you anything about what happened?"

"There wasn't much to tell. He said two guys in dark suits come in to the new gallery space. They didn't say anything. They just started beating him up. They knocked him out very briefly, and when Ted came to, the back wall of the gallery was on fire. He said there was something there on the floor like a Molotov cocktail, but he didn't know for sure because he's never actually seen a Molotov cocktail. Whatever it was, it started a fire."

"Some kind of incendiary device," Cat said. "Good that Ted managed to get out safely."

"With some help. The fire attracted attention from people on the street, and two guys he didn't know came in and pulled him out of the building. Someone else called the fire department and for an ambulance. That's about it. You were there when the ambulance took him away."

"And the two guys who beat him up?"

"Long gone. Ted had never seen them before. But here's the weird thing. When we got home from the hospital, I was helping him out of his clothes because they reeked of smoke. I found this piece of paper folded up in his jacket pocket. I gave it to him, and he read it. Ted said it was a threat. 'Drop this idea of doing business with the Chinese or you'll be very sorry.' He showed me the note."

"Oh, no. That's bad news."

"Yeah, really bad. We don't know what to do."

"Don't do anything right now. But keep your doors locked and be ready to call for help if you need it. Right now Ted needs to rest and recuperate and your job is to take care of him. I was going to call our police chief today, so I'll let him know about this. I have some additional information for him as well. And keep that note. It could be evidence."

"Thank you, Cat. You're a good friend."

"I'm going now. I'll call later and see how Ted is doing."

They said their goodbyes.

~~~

Cat could hear Miles entering the back door of the gallery.

"Don't let Greta come up here," she called out.

"Greta and Tito are eating breakfast over at the house. It's just me. I promise I won't knock anything over." She could hear Miles laughing.

"Come on up. I have things to tell you."

Miles came up the stairs into her office, pulled Cat up from her chair, hugged her and gave her a big kiss. "So what do you have to tell me?"

"I found Chen Associates. The dead woman is listed on their website as acquisitions office and wife of the CEO. Chen Associates sells both Chinese art and Native American art."

"Ah, I get the connections. So Sylvia didn't have a problem with stealing art, and Mateo didn't have a problem with killing her to get her out of the way because he has his own project he wants to do. And he's probably behind the attack on Ted Yang."
~~~

"Yep, that's what I think. So, Miles, how would you like to delay reading a book for a little while and go around with me to some of the galleries? I'd like to know if Mateo approached any other galleries. Maybe we can learn more about him."

"Yes, of course. My book can wait."

"Good. I suggest you go get some breakfast to eat then we'll do a little gallery tour."

Twenty minutes later, Cat and Miles took off on foot to visit as many galleries as they could. Before the morning was over, they had visited three galleries and talked to at least one person on the staff at each gallery. In all three cases, the gallerists said that they had been visited by a young Mexican or Mexican-American man who asked them the same questions that Mateo had asked Cat. Did they have any Chinese art? Did they have a business selling art online to Chinese collectors? All three of the gallerists had said no. They didn't know anything about selling Chinese art or selling to Chinese collectors. No, they didn't know the young man's name. But they did say that he had been accompanied by a man in a dark suit who appeared to be an employee or bodyguard.

Cat and Miles found crucial information at the fourth gallery. When Cat asked if they knew the name of the man who had approached them about Chinese art, the gallerist said, "He never introduced himself, but that man with him…the one who looked like a bodyguard…called him 'Señor Salazar' at one point." Cat thanked him and she and Miles left.

Outside in the street again, Cat said, "Excellent. Now we know his name. Mateo Salazar. Next we have to figure out who the hell he is and why he's causing all this trouble."

"Maybe your copper will know more about him," Miles said.

"Yes, Sam Morales is on my list to call. I'll ask him. And I'll call our attorney, Ana Hernandez. She'll want to know, too."

"But right now, can we go to Jillie's and get some lunch? I didn't eat much this morning and I'm starving," Miles said.

"Oh, I'm sorry. I should have fixed you a proper breakfast when you were in the shower."

"No problem. I like eating at Jillie's anyway."

Half an hour later, stomachs full, Miles said, "Want some ice cream?"

"No. I'm too full." Cat sat back in her chair and sighed. "Maybe we could go see Ted Yang this afternoon. Oh rats! I forgot to check my messages. Maybe Ted texted me." She pulled her cell phone out of her pocket and began scrolling messages.

Suddenly she sat up straight in the chair. "Oh, no! There's a series of texts from Fiona. She and Luca were abducted. They are being held in a house over in the Warren district." She handed the phone to Miles. He read the texts.

"Let's go home and get my car," Miles said. "You can call Sam Morales and see if he can meet us there."

"But where do we go?" Cat said as they rose, waved goodbye to Jillie, and began the walk home at a quick pace.

"Here's what you do, Cat. Google Bisbee, Arizona, then click on the map Google provides. Zoom into Warren. Then click on houses on different streets close to the ballpark. You'll get street addresses. Find the street with fourteen hundred addresses."

It only took Cat a couple of minutes. "I found it! Fourteen hundred block of Adrian Lane." Google is showing me a photo now of the house."

"Call your copper and give him the address."

Cat made the call. By that time, they'd arrived home. They jumped in the car and left immediately for Warren.

Ten minutes later, Cat and Miles met Police Chief Sam Morales and his deputy Dave Chapman outside the address 1403 Adrian Lane. Cat went upstairs and knocked on the front door. Miles banged on the garage door on the lower level.

All of them could hear Fiona and Luca calling out loudly. "Here! We're in here! Let us out!"

Chief Morales looked at the lock on the garage door. "Get that tire iron out of my squad car, Chapman. It's behind the driver's seat."

Deputy Chapman did as instructed and, within minutes, Morales had pried the entire lock off the garage door. He lifted the door. Fiona and Luca rushed out.

"Oh, thank god," Fiona said. "I was terrified those guys would come back before we could escape."

"Do you know who they are?" Sam Morales asked.

Fiona shook her head. She looked at Luca.

"They work for the Familia Tamaulipas cartel," Luca said.

"Oh, that's just great," Sam Morales said. "That's all we need – another Mexican cartel in Bisbee."

Suddenly, both Sam and Dave Chapman's radios began beeping loudly. Sam called in, listened to the dispatcher, and then turned to Cat.

"We have to go. There's some nutcase with a gun taking pot-shots at cars on the bypass.

Cat, take these two back to your house. Keep them there, and I'll connect with you later. Cat, enough investigating. Time to lay low now. Miles, try to keep Cat corralled."

Miles grinned and nodded. "With pleasure."

~~~

In the late afternoon, Trevor arrived back at Cat's house about the same time that Cat, Miles, Luca, and Fiona arrived. They all met around the kitchen table, sipping hot drinks.

Cat started the conversation. "Okay, let's talk to each other and fill in the gaps. I think we've identified that woman who stole the pot. She was Sylvia Chen. She was with a company in California that collects Chinese and Native American arts and crafts, and then tries to sell them to affluent Chinese collectors. As best we can determine, the white-suit man who threw her off the balcony and killed her is Mateo Salazar, a Mexican national who fancies himself a Chinese art expert. Looks like he wanted Sylvia Chen out of the way because he saw her as competition. And now he's trying to get Ted Yang out of the way, too. Ted is a client of mine
~~~

who is planning on opening a gallery here. He was beaten and his gallery set on fire. Do you think Mateo Salazar is the one who had you abducted?"

Fiona looked at Luca. "Do you want to tell them about you or shall I?"

Luca sighed. "I'm so sorry to cause such trouble."

Cat frowned. "What do you have to do with this, Luca? I don't understand. Why is Mateo Salazar coming after you?"

"Mateo is not the one coming after me. It's his sister, Victoria Salazar. Or, I should say, his half-sister. Their big brother was Jorge Salazar. All three siblings had the same father but a different mother."

Fiona spoke up. "Cat, remember the woman we saw back in the corner at the Star Tavern? That was Victoria Salazar."

"Ah…" Cat frowned. "That must be the mystery woman Renata heard talking to Mateo. Why does she want you, Luca?"

"I got involved with a woman named Camila who turned out to be Jorge Salazar's wife. Jorge was a *jefe* in the Familia Tamaulipas cartel."

"At first, Camila told him she was Jorge's daughter, not wife. She misled Luca," Fiona added.

Luca nodded. "Jorge found out she was unfaithful, and with me. Camila called me and told me to flee because he was going to kill me. She promised she would meet me later. So I went north and ended up in Bisbee. This was a little over a year ago."

"Did she follow you here? I don't remember you ever being with a woman," Cat said.

"No, Camila didn't make it here. Jorge executed her. Then, almost immediately, he had a heart attack and died. His sister, Victoria, blamed me for his death. She sent out word that she was coming for me, and she would make sure that I ended up dead just like her brother."

"Crikey," Trevor said. "This is like Borderlands crime-suspense movie."

"So you think Mateo had nothing to do with your abduction?" Cat asked.

"That's right. Camila told me that Mateo and Victoria never got along. He has his own project going on here. Victoria is here for me." Luca looked down, a frown on his face.

"Based on what Renata overheard," Cat said, "Victoria is upset with Mateo because she thinks he's getting in the way and attracting attention to her and her business activities. So it's even more complicated that we first realized."

"Victoria is after me, but I wouldn't be a bit surprised if she has some smuggling thing going on here as well," Luca added.

Miles nodded. "That's very possible. It's not unusual for cartels to attempt an expansion outside their regular territory. So you think Victoria took her brother's place in the cartel hierarchy?"

"That's very possible," Luca said. "I'm just sorry I didn't leave Bisbee earlier. I didn't want any of you, and especially you, Fiona, to become a target."

"Those two goons who abducted us are likely Victoria's men, not Mateo's. As far as we know, Mateo doesn't know about Luca, or maybe he doesn't care," Fiona added.

"But when those men return to the house in Warren and find you gone, they'll come looking for you," Cat said.

Trevor spoke up. "Sis, this is really worrying me. Mexican cartels are full of some really dangerous blokes. Do you think maybe it's time for you to go home?"

Miles spoke up. "If you want to leave right away, you can take my car. It's a rental. I plan to get my own car, but I haven't had time to look for a good deal. You won't be as easy to identify in a rental, and you can drop it off when you get to where you're going. The airport?"

"Thank you, Miles. Yes, I agree," Fiona said. "It's time for me to go home. And I'm taking Luca with me." She looked around the table. "But you can't tell anyone this. We want Victoria to think Luca ran away again, and no one knows where he is."

Everyone nodded.

"We'll leave tonight when it gets dark," Fiona added. "Luca, do you need anything from your apartment? They may be watching your place waiting for you to come home. Could you just get in the car with me and go?"

"I guess I could do without my violin. It's back in my apartment."

To Cat, Luca looked sad. "Anything else?" she asked.

"My passports. Yes, I will need the passports. It would be good to get some photos of my parents and my Mexican family. And some sheet music I was working on."

"You write music, too?" Fiona asked.

Luca nodded. "Mainly for cello. I usually play cello. The violin is for smaller venues, like art exhibit openings." He looked at Cat and smiled.

"The passports are absolutely crucial for Luca to travel outside the U.S. I have an idea about how we can get what you need," Miles said. "Trevor and I can go with you after dark on the trail up above Bisbee. We'll go into your place from the back in case they are watching for you to return. We won't turn on the lights. We can carry torches so you can find what you need. Then the three of us can carry backpacks with your most important things in them."

"We'll fix you some supper to take with you," Cat said.

"Sounds like a good plan," Fiona added. "Let's get the backpacks ready."

"And you'll stay here and not let anyone in, Cat?" Miles asked. He had a worried look on his face.

"I'll be good. And don't forget that I have these two mean, vicious Great Danes to protect me," Cat giggled.

"Tito will do his best to protect you," Miles answered. "I'm not so sure about Greta."

"Clumsy, goofy Greta will knock them down and lick their faces until they scream for mercy."

Miles grinned. "Yeah, mean, vicious Greta."

"Don't worry, Miles." Cat kissed him. "You boys go and hurry back."

~~~

While they were gone, Fiona packed up her things, and Cat made burritos ready to carry away in a bag and eat on the road. She added some *pan dulce, conchas* to be exact, some fruit, and bottles of water.

Fiona came and sat at the kitchen table with Cat. "Do you think I'm crazy?"

"For what?"

"For taking Luca back to England with me. I'll admit. I'm very attracted to him, but I don't really know him."

"My intuitive feeling about Luca is that he is a really good guy. He needs a family and a quiet life so he can write and play music. Fiona, I know a lot of artists. Many of them are kind of out of it and not that engaged with the world. That's because they are thinking about the next line on the paper, the next color on the canvas, the next word in the poem, the next note on the violin. They need love and stability so they can follow the art. I really think Luca is that kind of man. He follows the notes, and you follow the words. He'll flourish with you. And I bet you'll flourish with him."

Fiona nodded. "That's how I see him, too. He's suffered a lot of grief. I'd like to make Luca happy, and I think he'll make me happy. It's comforting to know you think the same."

They were quiet for a few minutes. Fiona spoke first. "Also, Luca told me something intriguing. When his lover Camila called to tell him to run away, he asked her to go with him. He was rightly worried about her safety. She said she'd meet him later. She said her husband would just beat her like he did the last time."

"The last time?" Cat was surprised. "That sounds like Camila may have engaged in an infidelity before Luca. Or maybe more than one."

"That's what I think," Fiona said. "That complicated every-thing."

The three men returned a few minutes later, backpacks full.
~~~

"I found an old cell phone," Luca said. "Those dudes took my new phone. But this old one needs charging."

"We can do that in the car," Fiona said.

"Right. There's a charger in the car," Miles said.

Cat looked at Luca and said, "Repeat after me, Luca."

He looked at her with a question on his face.

"I'm thinking of going to Canada. Maybe the west coast. It's very beautiful there."

Luca grinned and repeated her words.

Fiona added, "And you can tell Victoria that I said this: 'I'm meeting a friend in LA. We're going to drive up into the Sierra Nevada Mountains to see the giant sequoias.'"

Miles grinned. "Luca, these two women are very clever. Watch out or Fiona will wrap you around her little finger just like Cat did to me."

Luca smiled. "Too late. I'm already wrapped."

A few more minutes of organizing passed then Fiona stood in a circle with everyone. "I think it might be a good idea for me to send out a group text to you all as we make progress so you'll know we're safe. I think it's unlikely that Victoria or Mateo have the ability right now to hack into my phone and find out where we are. But I do want you to know that we're safe. At some point, I'll ditch the phone and get a new one."

"They may try to follow you," Miles said.

"Yes, but we'll be extra watchful and make sure we'll not being followed," she said.

"Cat, will you call Mari?" Luca asked. "Please tell her I had to leave, and I'm sorry that my departure was so abrupt. Thank her for everything."

Cat nodded. Her eyes filled with tears.

Everyone was quiet.

"Despite this rather bizarre exit, I want you to know that I had a great time," Fiona said. "I'll always remember Bisbee with great fondness. And, Trevor, I'll see you when you come home to London." Fiona went to Trevor, Miles, and Cat and hugged each one. "Thank you," she whispered to Cat.

Tears were rolling down Cat's cheeks now. Miles put his arm around her.

"I hope you can come back someday," Cat said.

"And I hope you come to visit us in London."

Luca shook hands with Miles and Trevor, and he hugged Cat. "You three are the best. The very best."

The lights were off in the front of the house. Miles went out on the front porch to make sure no cars were sitting in wait for them at the end of the street. He motioned when the coast was clear. He gave Fiona the keys to the rental car.

Fiona and Luca moved quietly out the front door, threw their packs and bags into the back seat of the car, and then they sat in front. They both waved goodbye. Then Fiona released the brake and rolled slowly down Cat's street. At the end of the street, she started the car's engine and turned on the headlights. She made a right turn onto Tombstone Canyon Road heading west. They disappeared into the dark night.

12 Confrontation

"Miles," Cat yawned and stretched. "Where are you, *cariño*?"

"I'm making coffee, *mi vida*. Get up, lazy girl." Miles turned and tossed a dog biscuit each to Tito and Greta, both lying near the back door.

Cat chuckled. Miles was beginning to use Spanish terms of endearment. Sweet. She plodded into the kitchen and plopped herself down at the table. Miles put a steaming cup of coffee in front of her.

"Where's Trevor?"

"He went birding with June early this morning, and this afternoon, he's going to soccer practice with Ana. I'd say Trevor is a bloke who is taking advantage of a promising situation."

"That's nice." Cat yawned again. "I'm having trouble waking up."

"I can see that. Drink your coffee. Here's something that will wake you up. I received a series of texts from Fiona starting last night. You got them, too. May I read them to you?"

"Yes, please." Cat began sipping the coffee.

"The first one came in about 9:30 p.m."

Picacho Peak is beautiful in the moonlight.

Cat smiled. "They bypassed Tucson and are heading for Phoenix."

The birds fly home at eight a.m. tomorrow from their harbor in the sky.

"Sky Harbor Airport, departure eight a.m. tomorrow. Or I guess that means this morning," Cat said. "They should be in the air right now."

The plan: Late lunch. Visit U.K. embassy for visa.

"I think she sent this one from the plane just before departure," Miles said. "They're headed for Washington, D.C. to get Luca a visa."

Will check in later.

"That's all from Fiona. But I got a personal text from Luca on that old cell phone he had," Miles said. "It came early this morning. You're going to love this."

"Really? What did he say?"

Miles. I'm so happy. I didn't know I could be this happy.

Miles looked up from his phone and grinned. "Here's the next one."

We couldn't leave last night so we got a motel room. I just spent the best night of my life with my beloved Fiona.

Cat giggled. "I wonder what they were doing all night."

"Oh, I can't imagine. I have *no* idea. No idea at all," Miles chuckled. "Next text."

I'm so in love. Fiona is the THE ONE. She's THE ONE I've been looking for my entire life.

"He has 'the one' all in caps," Miles grinned.

Downside. When I first turned on this phone, there was a message from Victoria. She said she's looking for me.

"Hmmm…." Miles frowned.

I'm going to smash this phone and throw it out in the desert. This is my last message to you until I arrive HOME.

"He has 'home' in all caps," Miles said.

"Luca means England when he says 'home.'"

"Last message."

Deepest love and gratitude to you and Cat. Luca.

"That's so sweet," Cat said.

Suddenly there was a loud knock at the front door of Cat's house. Cat peeked around to see who was there.

"Miles, that's Sam Morales. Please go let him in, and I'll get dressed."

Miles, accompanied by the two dogs, went through the living room and opened the front door.

"Hi, Sam, come on in. Cat is getting dressed. Let's go in the kitchen, and I'll get you a cup of coffee." He noticed that Sam was in his police uniform with a gun in its holster strapped at his side

"Sounds good. My deputy dropped me off. My squad car is making god-awful clanking noises, and I don't dare trust it anymore. The damn thing went straight to the mechanic." He reached out and petted two dog heads simultaneously, which brought on vigorous tail wagging. "Tito, Greta," he said. "Good doggies."

Sam followed Miles into the kitchen and sat at the table. Cat joined them almost immediately.

"Here's your coffee. Need any milk or sugar?" Miles asked.

"No thanks, I like it black."

"Hey, I heard you were going on a vacation." Cat said. "Why are you still here?"

"Too much going on now. But as soon as I get a break, my wife and I are taking the kids to Disneyland. It's in Anaheim in the LA area." Sam took a sip and looked at Cat. "Can you catch me up? There are gaps in the narrative here. What do you know?"

"First," Cat asked, "did you talk to Renata Romero a second time? She remembered quite a bit more after she first talked to you."

"Yes, I did talk to her a second time."

"I think the most important thing I've discovered has been names. First the dead woman is Sylvia Chen." Cat told Sam about Chen Associates and how Sylvia was listed as an "acquisition agent."

"So her role was to find Chinese artifacts and then her company would sell them?"

"Yes, sell them to rich Chinese collectors. And her company also sells Native American arts and crafts. We're pretty sure she stole that pot from Michael and Willow."

"And the man in the white suit who probably killed her?"

"Remember Renata overhearing that conversation in which the name Mateo was used?"

"Yes."

"Miles and I found out that his last name is Salazar. He's a Mexican national. We've been able to piece together that his plan is to create a business similar to the Chen's but based here in Bisbee. Sylvia Chen was in his way."

"So Salazar eliminated the competition. And that means he probably was behind the beating of Ted Yang and the torching of Yang's gallery. We're investigating that now," Sam said. "We stumbled upon his name, too."

Cat nodded. "Mateo Salazar came to my gallery and tried to find out if I was in the same business, too. I made it clear that I have no interest in being an agent selling Chinese artifacts to affluent Chinese collectors. I did *not* tell him that I was working for Ted Yang as his graphic designer."

"We also are learning more about Mateo Salazar," Sam said. "The Cochise County Sheriff's Department is involved in the investigation, too. Salazar may be telling people that this is all about art, but we think it's a money laundering scheme. I mean, turning drug money into art money."

"That I know nothing about," Cat said, "but I would not be a bit surprised to learn he's into money laundering. Do you know Luca Sutherland?"

"He works for Mari Spencer, right? Handyman? Is he causing trouble, too?"

"No," Cat said, "on the contrary, he's trying to get away from trouble. Remember the mystery woman Renata told you about who was very critical of Mateo Salazar's China-related business idea?"

"Yes, do you know who she is and what's she got to do with Luca Sutherland?"

"Her name is Victoria Salazar. She's Mateo's older sister, and she's also Jorge Salazar's younger sister. How this relates to Luca is that he had an affair with a woman who was married to Jorge Salazar."

"Oh, crap. Jorge is a boss in La Familia Tamaulipas cartel."

"*Was*. He's dead now. Jorge's wife, Camila, told Luca that she was Jorge's daughter, not his wife. Luca discovered later that she was really his wife. When Jorge Salazar found out about their affair, he killed Camila. He was planning on going after Luca and kill him, too, but Salazar died suddenly of a heart attack. Luca had gone on the run, and he ended up in Bisbee. Jorge's sister Victoria blamed Luca for her brother Jorge's death so she decided to find Luca, and take her revenge on him by killing him."

"Wait a minute. Jorge was the cartel boss. His sister is Victoria, and Jorge had an even younger brother, Mateo? So this is some kind of family drama." Sam shook his head.

"Exactly. Luca told us that all three siblings had different mothers. Apparently Victoria and Jorge were close. But Victoria and Mateo are most definitely not close."

Sam was quiet for a moment. "So there are two things going on here. Mateo wants to start up some business about Chinese art that could involve money-laundering. And Victoria wants to kill Luca Sutherland as an act of revenge."

"You got it," Cat said.

"If that weren't bad enough, I think there's even more to this than you have already discovered, Cat. And I have to say, I'm pretty impressed by what you've learned." Sam reached out and patted her hand. "Sure you don't want to be a police officer?" He grinned.

"Thanks, Sam. But no thanks on the job offer. I'm happy doing what I do."

"Let me explain what we think is going on. Imagine a map of southern Arizona and the state of Sonora just south of Arizona."

"I have a map," Mile said. "Just a minute and I'll get it." He left the kitchen and quickly returned. Miles spread the map open on the kitchen table.

Sam pointed to the far eastern border of Arizona where it met the New Mexico border. "This area in Mexico just south of the U.S. state of New Mexico and farther east is controlled by the Sinaloa cartel. The area west of Nogales, Sonora, and just south of Nogales, Arizona, also is controlled by Sinaloa. But this area in between Nogales, Arizona, and the New Mexico border, which includes Bisbee and Douglas, is primarily controlled by Cártel Jalisco Nueva Generación. We'll just call them Jalisco for short."

Miles was frowning now. "I bet there's ongoing conflict between Jalisco and Sinaloa for this contested area so close to us."

"Yes," Sam said. "There have been several shoot-outs between Sinaloa and Jalisco gangs in Nogales, in Agua Prieta just south of Douglas, Arizona, and even in Naco, Sonora, just south of Naco, Arizona."

"Wow. That really is close to us here in Bisbee," Cat said.

Sam sighed. "If that weren't enough, our informants are telling us that a third cartel is trying to take advantage of this upheaval. The third cartel is trying to move into this contested area and take it over."

Miles said, "Don't tell me. Familia Tamaulipas cartel?"

"Exactly," Sam said. "Familia Tamaulipas is engaged in the same smuggling business as Jalisco and Sinaloa. We heard just recently that one of the Tamaulipas *jefes* died suddenly."

"Jorge Salazar?" Cat asked.

"That's what we think. Then we heard that his sister was taking over his role in the cartel."

"Victoria Salazar?"

Sam nodded. "Yep. Too many coincidences."

Cat frowned. "So Victoria's concern with Mateo was more than his just being a dumbass getting involved in the Chinese art market. She thought his antics might interfere with her real goal which is to take over this section of the border and her on-going efforts to smuggle drugs into Arizona."

"That's what we think," Sam said. "I'll add that we think both Victoria and Mateo are very dangerous."

"Luca is gone now. He left Bisbee last night with Fiona Davies. She's a visiting travel writer who was here for a few days. Her brother, Trevor, is staying with us now," Miles explained.

"So Luca is on the run again?" Sam Morales asked.

"Yes," Cat added. "He knew Victoria was here to get him. I don't think he knew anything about Mateo's projects or about this cartel competition. My impression of Luca is that he just wants to play music and have a peaceful life. He wants to survive."

"Then he's going to have to go pretty far away to escape these *pendejos*," Sam said.

"Fiona will take care of that," Miles said. "They are on their way to the U.K. Don't tell anyone."

Sam smiled. "I'm glad to hear that Sutherland made it out of here. So now I need to turn my attention to Mateo and Victoria. We've been looking for them both. We know Victoria has been here, but we haven't been able to find her. More important for us now is to find Mateo Salazar. He's a murder suspect, and we want to arrest him but we haven't been able to find him either."

Suddenly there was a loud knocking at the front door. Cat got up and walked into the living room. Tito and Greta followed her. Through the glass, she could see two men standing there. One appeared to be Mateo Salazar, and the other, his bodyguard. "Miles," she whispered loudly.

Cat cracked the door open. "What do you want?" she said.

"Now, don't be unfriendly, Miss Miranda." Salazar shoved his shoulder hard against the door and both men pushed into Cat's living room.

Cat was forced to step back. Tito took one look at the two men and moved his big body in front of Cat to protect her.

When the bodyguard saw Tito, he pulled a gun from his suit-coat jacket and pointed it at Tito.

"You better not hurt my dog," Cat said loudly.

"Or what?" Salazar laughed.

"Or you'll have to deal with me," Miles said from the kitchen door. "Put that gun away." Miles glanced over at Sam who was standing now next to the kitchen table. Sam was pulling his gun out of its holster.

"I told you. I am not dealing in Chinese art," Cat said.

"Look, Miss Miranda, I'm not here to bother your dogs, and I'm not here to talk about Chinese art. My sister Victoria wants me to bring Luca Sutherland to her." He smiled what had to be the most insincere smile Cat had ever seen.

"So now you are your sister's errand boy?" Cat asked in a sarcastic tone.

A flash of anger lit up Mateo Salazar's eyes. His fake smile disappeared. "Shut up and tell me where to find Sutherland."

"I have no idea where he is."

"I don't believe you. Tell me or else you'll pay a heavy price." He gestured to the body guard who pointed the gun now at Cat.

"Put that gun down!" Miles said in a loud voice.

At just that moment, Police Chief Sam Morales moved from out of sight in the kitchen to stand beside Miles. He took a classic law enforcement stance, holding his gun in both hands, and pointed it at Salazar's bodyguard.

"Drop the gun. *Now!*" Sam demanded.

The bodyguard had a panicked look on his face. He looked over at Mateo Salazar.

Mateo growled and grabbed Cat. He jerked her up against him, roughly turned her around to face Miles, and he held her close to his body. His right arm was around her midsection and his left hand was tight against her throat.

Tito did not like this. He jumped up and attempted to take Salazar's right arm into his jaws. The bodyguard lifted his gun and pointed it at Tito. He pulled the trigger. Tito yelped in pain and fell down to the floor, blood coming from a wound in his side.

"You bastard!" Cat yelled.

"Drop the gun!" Sam Morales shouted a second time.

The bodyguard turned instead and pointed the gun at Cat. That was too much for Sam Morales. He pulled the trigger, and the bodyguard went down, blood streaming from his upper chest.

By this time, Miles had jumped forward and grabbed Salazar's arm just enough for Cat to jump free of his hold. That was all it took. Miles began to viciously punch Mateo Salazar. He punched and kicked Salazar until the man was curled into a knot on the floor, groaning in pain.

Cat pulled Miles away. "Everything's okay, Miles. We're okay now," she whispered.

Meanwhile, Sam Morales came forward and took the gun from the bodyguard's limp hand. Holding his gun on the bodyguard, he took a quick look. "He'll need to go to the ER but this isn't a wound that will kill him." Sam stepped back and reached for a police radio attached to his belt. He called for backup and for an ambulance.

"Miles, do you have any of those plastic ties or some rope or something?" Sam asked. "I'll put my handcuffs on Salazar, but I still need something to hold this other dude."

"No problem, Sam. I'll be right back." Miles went into the kitchen and returned a minute later with the plastic ties. Sam already handcuffed Salazar. Now he pulled the bodyguard's hands behind his back and tied him. The bodyguard groaned in pain.

"Are you hurt?" Miles asked Cat. He pulled her into his arms.

"No, I'm just fine. Let's look at Tito. We have to take him to the veterinarian's office."

Cat and Miles both went to Tito. Cat began to stoke his head as she told him what a good boy he was.

Sam took a look, too. "Looks like a superficial wound to me. He'll need to be cleaned up, maybe get some stitches, and some antibiotics."

The sound of sirens came closer.

"Good," said Sam. "Pretty fast response."

Cat glanced over at Greta. The big puppy had crawled behind the couch. She was trembling all over, and she had a wild, terrified look in her eyes. A whimper escaped her throat when Cat looked at her.

"Oh, you poor baby," Cat said. "You're not the warrior that Tito is, are you? That's okay. Your calling is to make people feel better, not to bite them and make them drop their guns."

Sam's deputy, Dave Chapman, arrived first. He entered the house just as the ambulance and two Cochise County deputies arrived in a police van.

"Whoa. Lots of excitement here, Chief," Chapman said.

"Yeah, these two dudes are real trouble makers. The good news is that we can arrest both of them. Pull Salazar up to his feet."

Deputy Chapman complied. Mateo Salazar stared at Sam Morales, an intensely hostile scowl on his face.

Sam Morales informed Mateo Salazar that he was being arrested for assaulting Catalina Miranda and on suspicion of the murder of Sylvia Chen. He read Salazar his rights. Mateo said nothing.

"Okay, we'll turn Salazar over to the Cochise County deputies," Sam said. "They can take him directly to jail." Two deputies came forward and moved Salazar into their van.

Morales looked at the wounded bodyguard now on an ambulance stretcher. "Chapman, drop me off at our office, and then you go with this man to the hospital. Make sure he stays put. We'll turn him over to the Sheriff's Department later."

"You bet," Chapman said. He and Sam followed the ambulance team out.

Sam turned back and said to Cat, "Stay in touch."

"Thank you so, so much, Sam." Cat blew him a kiss. Police Chief Sam Morales laughed.

Miles said, "Cat, do you have a wheel barrow?"

"Yes, it's in that storage shed in the back. Why do you need a wheel barrow?"

"To carry Tito to your car. I'm afraid he's too big and too heavy for me to carry very far on my own."

Cat smiled. "I'll go get it." She appeared at the backdoor a couple of minutes later. "It's too big. I can't get it in the backdoor."

Miles crouched down next to the big Great Dane, put his arms around Tito while trying to encompass both the dog's shoulders and hips. Tito began to struggle. He whimpered in pain. "Be still, Tito." This was a command that Tito had been taught by Miles's dad Ian Trevelyan when Ian, Amanda, and Tito went bird watching. Tito grew still. Miles struggled and finally was able to lift Tito into his arms. He stood and carried the dog to the wheelbarrow.

"He's so heavy, and he's so big," Miles groaned.

"You're doing great, Miles. Greta, come here, baby." Cat leashed Greta, and Miles wheeled Tito to Cat's car. Cat called their vet's office to warn them that they were coming.

"Greta can get in the back seat. I'll lift the hatchback and put Tito in the far back," Miles said.

Soon all four of them were in place, and Miles drove them to the vet's office.

13 A Conversation

"Where do I go?" Miles asked. "I've never been to the vet's office."

"San Jose district. We're going to Dr. Kumar's office. She's seen Tito earlier for his check up and vaccinations. Your dad took Greta there, too."

When they arrived at the office, Miles noticed the name at the entrance. Dr. Amisha Kumar. "Is he Indian?" Miles asked.

"He is a she, and yes, her parents emigrated from India," Cat explained. "She was born and grew up in Arizona. Her name is Amisha but she goes by the name Amy. She married a local man from Bisbee, and they have a couple of kids."

Miles carried Tito to the examination room while Cat checked them in at the front desk. Dr. Kumar came in immediately. She was a slender woman in her late thirties with long dark hair wrapped in a knot at the nape of her neck. She was dressed in a white coat with a stethoscope around her neck.

"I'm Dr. Kumar," she said to Miles. Her attention went right to Tito.

"Oh, my sweet big boy," she said in a gentle voice. Tito's tail began to wag.

Cat came into the room with Greta on the leash. "Hey, Amy. This total butthead shot Tito. Well, not really. The bullet didn't go in."

"Well, I hope the shooter got in big trouble."

"Sam Morales took care of him. He's in the Cochise County Jail now."

"Good."

"Oh, this is *mi novio* Miles Trevelyan."

"Dr. Kumar," Miles nodded.

"Nice to meet you. Call me Amy." She turned her attention to Tito and began her examination.

Tito whined in pain and wagged his tail at the same time.

"Okay. This wound isn't so bad. As you said, the bullet did not go in so the wound is superficial. I'll give him a sedative first." Tito got his injection and began to doze off almost immediately. Dr. Kumar used an electric razor to shave away the fur around the wound. She quickly stitched up the wound with six neat stitches. Then she reached into a cabinet and pulled out a small bottle of pills which she handed to Cat.

"Does Tito like peanut butter?"

"He loves peanut butter," Cat said.

"Then put the antibiotic pill in a spoonful of peanut butter. He'll swallow the pill without even realizing it. Give him all the pills starting today. One each day."

"I'll give some peanut butter to Greta, too, so she won't feel left out."

On their way out, Dr. Kuman said, "Also, here's the plastic cone to put around Tito's neck. That will keep him from tearing out the stitches with his teeth. He's going to be sore for a while, but he'll be better sooner than you think." She handed the plastic cone to Cat. Then she reached out and stroked Greta's head. "And my sweet Greta. You take care of Tito. Okay?"

Greta wagged her tail.

Nearly two hours later, they returned home again. Miles carried Tito in, groaning and complaining the entire time about how heavy the dog was. Miles put Tito on his bed, and Cat put the plastic cone around his neck. Tito stayed asleep the entire time.

"He's not going to like wearing the Cone of Shame," Cat chuckled. "But it won't be for long."

"Tito is going to be fine. Greta is going to be fine, too. The vet office staff made such a big fuss over her," Miles said. "I think it would be easy to spoil Greta."

They fell silent, holding hands and watching the dogs nap on their big floor pillows.

"Best of all," Cat said, "Mateo Salazar and his goon are in jail now. All is well." Cat paused. "Oh, I guess not totally well."

"No? What's wrong?" Miles asked.

"You haven't kissed me since forever."

He laughed. "I can fix that."

Several hours later, Cat and Miles were lying in bed holding each other when Miles's phone beeped. Miles reached for it.

"It's a text from Fiona."

"What does she say?" Cat asked.

Visa acquired. On the way by train to NYC LaGuardia. Will message you from Heathrow.

Cat grinned. "Good! Very good."

Miles nodded. "Except for one problem. You haven't kissed me since forever."

"Oh, *pobrecito*. Come here, Miles Trevelyan." Cat reached for him.

~~~

The next morning, Miles helped Tito out to the backyard to pee, helped him to get a drink of water, and then helped the big dog back to his bed.

"He's still really sleepy. I'll try to feed him later. Right now, I'm going to take Greta for a run."

"Do your best to wear her out, Miles. We don't want her pestering Tito. I'm opening the gallery this morning around eleven a.m., and I have a couple of small paintings to hang. I need to sweep the floor, too, and tidy up before the art opening tomorrow evening."

"See you later." Miles and Greta left and quickly disappeared, running toward the hillside trail above Cat's house.
~~~

Cat called Ted Yang and spoke to him for a few minutes. She told him about the arrest of Mateo Salazar and his bodyguard. "Sam Morales thinks Salazar is the one behind the attack on you, and also for the fire in your new gallery."

"This is such great news, Cat. To know they are all in jail is such a relief."

"What about you? What are your plans?"

"I'm going ahead with my plans. It's going to take a while to get the gallery in shape. But I'm recovering really fast from that beating they gave me. I actually feel pretty positive about the future. Jessie is helping me."

"Good. So do you want me to go ahead with your website design?"

"Yes. Definitely."

They chatted a few more minutes. Then Cat and Ted Yang said their goodbyes.

Cat was still sitting at the kitchen table drinking coffee and making notes about the next art opening when she heard a knock at her front door. She went to the front of the house and looked out of the window.

There was a woman there. A wave of alarm went through Cat's body. The woman was Victoria Salazar.

Cat opened the door slightly. "Yes?"

"Miss Miranda. I am Victoria Salazar. May I come in and speak with you for a few moments?"

Cat hesitated. "Are you alone?"

"Yes, quite alone. My employees are assigned elsewhere."

Cat opened the door wider and stepped aside. She noticed the elegant suit and silk blouse that Victoria Salazar wore, including fashionable spike heels and expensive-looking jewelry. Her dark hair was arranged in a complicated French roll. She carried a small purse, too, made of some kind of leather. Her English was excellent with only the hint of a Spanish-speaker's accent.

"Please sit down," Cat said in a formal tone. "Would you care for some coffee?"

"I appreciate your hospitality, but no. I just drank a cup."

"What can I do for you?"

"I don't know how much you know about my family's history. I am the younger sister of Jorge Salazar who passed away last year from a heart attack. He experienced a trauma that caused extreme stress, which led to the heart attack."

Cat nodded. "I'm sorry for your loss."

"I'll be frank. I've come to take Luca Sutherland back to Mexico City and make him pay for causing my beloved brother's death. I think you know where Luca can be found."

Cat looked directly into her eyes. "He left. He left Bisbee."

"Where did he go?" Victoria had a slight smile on her face, but Cat could see the annoyance in her eyes.

"I don't know."

"Really? You really don't know?" Clearly, Victoria Salazar did not believe Cat. "It's in your interest to tell me the truth."

Again, Cat looked at her directly. Cat knew that if she looked to the side or down, or if she hesitated, Victoria Salazar would know that she was lying.

"My interest?"

"I pay well for good information."

"Ah. Too bad for me because I really don't know where he is."

"He said nothing to indicate where he might go after leaving Bisbee?"

Cat hesitated. "I don't want to be a party in some act of revenge."

"You will not be involved, and no one will know what you told me."

Cat waited a long moment.

"Just before he left, Luca said he was thinking of going to Canada. To the west coast of Canada. He said it was beautiful there. But he did not say where exactly he planned to go."

Victoria sat back. "Probably Vancouver."

Cat shrugged. "He did not mention Vancouver. But before you go looking for him, I think there's something you should know."

Victoria Salazar's eyes narrowed.

"It was your men who abducted him and the British woman, right?"

She nodded.

"While they were together in that house, and before Sam Morales and his deputy freed them, Luca told the British woman some interesting things about his interactions with the Salazar family. And later she told me."

Cat was being really careful now about what she said. True, it was Fiona that had taken her aside and told Cat some of the details about Luca's affair with Camila Salazar. But Cat did not want Victoria Salazar to know Fiona's name or anything about her.

"And what are these 'interesting things'?" Victoria asked.

"Luca Sutherland said that he was approached and aggressively pursued by a woman named Camila Salazar when he was working at a seaside resort playing with his musical group."

Victoria frowned. "Go on."

"This woman, Camila, seduced Luca, and they became lovers. And here's the interesting part. She told Luca that she was the daughter of Jorge Salazar. She told him that she and Luca had to keep their affair a secret because her father would not approve of her relationship with a poverty-stricken musician."

The look of annoyance on Victoria's face had turned into fury. Her face was now a dark red color.

Cat continued. "It wasn't until much later that Luca learned the truth. His lover, Camila, was married to Jorge Salazar. She was his wife, not his daughter."

Victoria said nothing. Her face was still red, and she was clicking her long, painted nails against the wooden arm of the chair.

"Based on some things Camila said, Luca was not the first of her infidelities. Apparently, Camila had been unfaithful more than once. So it seems that Jorge wasn't the only one who was cheated," Cat added. "Luca was cheated, too."

"*Puta barata*," Victoria growled. Cheap whore.

The two women sat in silence for a long moment.

"I understand your concern for your brother Jorge," Cat finally said. "I also was close to my brother. He died nearly two years ago. I will always miss him." She hesitated. "But in your case, I think you would be wasting your time going after Luca Sutherland. It appears to me that your little brother Mateo is the one who is causing you problems now."

Victoria looked sharply at Cat. "He was arrested and now he's in the Cochise County jail. I'm going to see that he gets a good lawyer. But he created this dreadful mess. There's not a lot I can do for him. And there's not a lot I *want* to do for him."

"I take it that you are not close with Mateo?"

"He's been a thorn in my side since his childhood. His mother was a spoiled, arrogant, selfish bitch, and she raised her precious son to be spoiled, arrogant, and selfish, too. For his entire life, Mateo has assumed that the world owes him whatever he wants. He has a history of doing really stupid things in his pursuit of his always stupid goals."

"Like killing people," Cat said.

Victoria Salazar shrugged. "He went to China as a tourist. He was there about a month, traveling around, and he came home with this ridiculous idea of marketing Chinese art. He knows nothing about Chinese art. Or about marketing art."

"And then he systematically began to eliminate anyone who got in his way," Cat said.

Victoria's nod was a small, tight gesture.

"And now he is interfering with your business?" Cat asked.

Victoria looked directly at Cat.

"You are a clever woman, Cat Miranda. "What have you heard about me?"

"This is a small town, and people pay attention to what happens on both sides of the border. I've heard that you are in the import business."

Victoria Salazar smiled. "Yes, imports."

Smuggling in other words, Cat thought to herself.

Cat continued. "But you have two chief competitors who are in intense conflict over this section of the border region. Word is that you hoped to take advantage of their difficult relationship and move into the void with your own business."

"Yes, that was the plan. Actually, I hoped to negotiate a deal with both of these competitors."

"But Mateo screwed everything up. He drew attention to you and your business dealings before you could make any progress on your goals."

Victoria nodded. "As usual. He manages always to do the wrong thing. And while doing the wrong thing, he constantly badgers me for money."

Cat sat quietly. Victoria was coming to the only logical conclusion. Forget about Luca. Mateo was her real problem.

Victoria Salazar's face changed suddenly. She looked at Cat with an evaluative gaze.

"As I said, you are a very clever woman. I wonder if you'd be interested in working for me. I could use a reliable manager in my import business. It would mean relocating to the Rio Grande Valley on the border between Texas and Mexico, probably to Matamoros in the state of Tamaulipas. You would be responsible for managing personnel as well as shipments."

Cat took a deep breath. She decided to play along.

"And what would be my reward for this new endeavor?"

"You will be very well paid for your efforts. If things go well, you will also get large bonuses."

Cat sat in silence for a long moment. She took another deep breath, looked at Victoria directly, and said, "Thank you for your generous offer. However, you should know that my beloved brother, Luis, the brother I mentioned earlier, left his gallery and this house to me in his will. Luis had a life goal of introducing and promoting artists in this region, and especially Bisbee artists. I decided to take up his life goal and make it mine. Also, I have a love relationship with a man who could not move so easily. He's a professor at the University of Arizona in Tucson."

Victoria smiled. "I see. And I understand. This is your home, your life's work is here, and you have ties here that you do not want to break."

"Exactly. My brother Luis would want me to stay here. *Mi novio* would want the same."

"I understand."

At that moment, Miles and Greta came bounding into the kitchen through the backdoor. Miles stripped his wet t-shirt off, and Greta went directly to her water bucket where she began noisily slurping water.

"Cat? Where are you?" Miles called out.

"In the living room."

Miles walked into the living room. He was dressed in tight jogging shorts. His blonde hair was tousled, his face was pink, his blue eyes bright, and his chest bare. His muscles flexed as he walked into the living room. As far as Cat was concerned, he was about as good looking as a human male could possibly be.

"Oh, I'm sorry. You have a guest," Miles said.

"Victoria, this is *mi novio*, Miles Trevelyan. Miles, this is Victoria Salazar."

"Nice to meet you," he said.

Victoria nodded.

"It's okay for you to go and shower now," Cat said. She smiled.

"Excuse me, then," Miles said.

Victoria turned to Cat. "I quite understand why you wouldn't want to leave behind this man. *Muy guapo.*" She smiled.

"Yes, *muy guapo.* Very handsome. And he's a wonderful lover."

Greta entered the room and headed straight for Victoria Salazar. The woman sat back in her chair, alarmed now.

"This is Greta," Cat said. "She's friendly."

Greta came to stand next to Victoria. She put her head in Victoria's lap and looked up at her with a soulful look.

Cat blinked, amazed at Greta's behavior. "Greta wants you to be happy," Cat said. "She puts her head in people's laps when she thinks they are sad and when they need some cheering up."

Victoria relaxed slightly and nodded. She stroked Greta's head. "Very sweet." After a moment, she stood and moved toward the door. Greta sat down next to Cat. "Thank you for speaking with me," she said.

Cat stood also. "Thank you for your job offer. I appreciate it. But I will stay here and be happy. I hope you will be happy, too."

"And I will return to Matamoros. I will send a lawyer to Mateo, and let him work out his own destiny. And I think you are correct about Luca Sutherland. He is not worthy of my time. It seems that Camila was the true villain and the one responsible for my brother's death."

Victoria Salazar left Cat's home. She waited at the bottom of the stairs for less than a minute. Then a dark-suited man wearing dark sunglasses and driving a dark BMW appeared. Victoria got into the car and they drove away.

Miles reappeared a few minutes later.

"Boy, do I have a story to tell you," Cat said.

"I was worried about leaving you with her, but you seemed to be okay."

"Yes. But…" she grinned. "But you'd better never show up half naked like that again, or you'll have *two* women jumping on you!"

Miles laughed. "I'll remember that. Tell me your story."

~~~

Later that evening, Cat and Miles sat out in the backyard near a metal fire ring where Miles had started a small fire.

"This smells so good," Miles said.

"You used mesquite wood to build the fire. Mesquite smoke always smells good," Cat replied.

"Cat, I want to ask you about Victoria Salazar. Do you think you really convinced her not to go after Luca? And is she really giving up her plan to start a smuggling operation here? I guess I'm worrying about this."

Cat nodded. "I was concerned, too. But the more I think about it, what Victoria is doing makes sense. It's clear that Mateo is a
~~~

pain in her side, and she'd be better off going back to her own territory where she can control outcomes without worrying about his interference. She is, after all, a serious businesswoman. Other than sending Mateo a lawyer to handle his case, she's left him to his fate."

"I see what you mean. Her business plan here wasn't working out."

"And I think her business plan has been her real priority all along, not Luca."

"So he's off the hook?"

"Very likely. I also think, although we'll never know for sure, that Camila Salazar was a repeat offender."

"You mean Luca wasn't the only one she had an affair with?"

"Yeah. I bet she had strayed multiple times. Jorge got fed up with the repeated humiliations and decided to get rid of her in a very public way. When I told Victoria that Camila had claimed to be Jorge's daughter, I could see that information really infuriated Victoria. I think she already knew, or at least suspected, that Camila couldn't keep her panties on. Victoria called her a *puta barata*."

"Whoa. That's pretty strong language."

"Yes, but Victoria knowing this made her realize that Luca was not to blame. Camila was the problem. We'll never know for sure, but my bet is that she's dismissed Luca as a concern. I doubt she'll even look for him in Vancouver."

"Or London."

"Especially London. Too far away. Not worth the trouble." Cat smiled. "We'll leave Luca to Fiona."

"And I fully expect Fiona will keep him busy."

Cat giggled. "And will you keep me busy, Señor Miles?"

"Very busy." Miles leaned over and kissed her. Suddenly his phone beeped. He reached for it.

"It's an email from Fiona."

"Read it!" Cat said. "Where are they?"

Miles, Luca and I arrived at Heathrow safely. We're both worn out. We'll collect our luggage then go to my flat. I'll email you soon. Best to you and Cat, Fiona.

"Excellent," Cat said. "Excellent."

14 Epilogue

Mid-January

Cat sat at the kitchen table, and she stared at the pile of seed catalogs in front of her. Greta was standing next to her, with her big Great Dane head in Cat's lap.

"You're trying to make me feel better, aren't you, Greta?"

Greta wagged her tail.

"I'm sad because Miles is leaving later this afternoon. He's going back to Tucson, and he has to start teaching again. I know he'll be back on Friday, but I still feel sad. I'm going to miss him. I always miss him when he's gone."

"Hey, Cat," Miles called from his library-office. The room was actually a bedroom that they had converted into a space for Miles to write his books. The walls were lined with bookshelves full of books, and a desk with a computer was prominent against one wall.

"Can you come in here, please? I received an email from Fiona. I want to read it to you."

"Coming." Greta, and fully-recovered Tito, too, followed Cat. She sat down in a chair next to Miles at his desk.

"Ready?"

Cat nodded.

Hello Miles. I'm emailing you because I'm not entirely sure Cat has escaped the attention of the cartel operatives in northern Mexico. I fear her email may get hacked and someone will see that she knows me and she has hidden some information from them. I don't want to get her in any trouble, and/or us, too. Since you and I are still on the U.K. system, I think writing to you will be less problematic until we all feel safer. This email will be long because I have a lot to share. Please make sure Cat gets to read it, too.

Luca and I have been here for about a month, not that long really. Sometimes it seems like yesterday that we arrived at Heathrow, collected our luggage, made our way to the Underground station and rode all the way home. I live in the Earl's Court area of Kensington in west central London. My flat has two bedrooms. I had a roommate to share expenses, but she moved out shortly before I left for my U.S. and Mexico tour. So it's just Luca and me now.

Yes, it seems like yesterday that we arrived. And yet, it feels like we've been here forever, and Luca and I have known each other forever. I'm so lucky to know him. We are very comfortable with each other. Tell Cat that she was quite correct in her assessment of Luca. He is the sweetest, kindest man I have ever known. He's what they call "laid back" or "chilled." He was looking for a home and for someone to love and to love him. He's found that now with me. He's always cheerful. He tells me every day that he loves me and that he's happier than he's ever been in his life. Truthfully, that's how I feel, too. Happy. Content. Serene.

Luca takes this all in his stride, as if we were meant to be. Not I. For me, this is all amazing. Sort of a miracle. I never expected to find a man like Luca. But here he is. I am so, so in love with Luca Sutherland. I'm totally chuffed to be here with him.

Luca and I share one bedroom, and I helped him take over the second bedroom and turn it into a music room. I have two desks with two computers where I work. One desk is in our bedroom, and the other is in our living room. I go back and forth between the two depending on what I'm working on. One computer location is for nonfiction freelance writing. The other computer location is for fiction. That sounds a bit bonkers, but it works for me.

I'm well into writing the travel book I told you about. It focuses on art and food in the American Southwest. So many travel books focus on the natural beauty of the American West with spots like the Grand Canyon and the red rock country of Utah. That's as it should be. But I wanted to take a different approach. So it's art and food for me. The book has a lot about different art destinations, and best places to eat. I'm adding cultural information, too. Actually I consider food to be an art in this book. Bisbee will have its own chapter. I'm blogging on this topic, too, and I've written several travel articles as well. Two articles have already been accepted for publication.

Also, I'm working on two novels. One is science fiction, or really it's more speculative fiction than a space opera sci-fi book. The other book is a time-travel romance. LOL. I never thought I'd write something like that. I'm not going to say more. I don't want to jinx the writing process.

Luca's music room is full of violins, a cello, a viola, a guitar, a small electronic keyboard, shelves full of sheet music, and a desk where Luca writes his music. He has applied for entry into the Royal College of Music, and he already found a group in our neighbourhood to play with at a nearby pub. He's already accepted a student who comes once a week for cello lessons. She's the daughter of a Mexican diplomat, so they speak Spanish with each other during the lesson. The pub gig and teaching cello means he's making some money already.

One more thing. When we arrived home, Luca and I decided that we needed a pet. We decided against a dog because we both have really busy schedules, and I know we'll be travelling again, too. A dog would get lonely. So we went to the animal shelter with the intent to get a cat. We came home with two cats! They are still kittens, not from the same litter, and they are very active. They play together constantly, zipping around the flat at top speed. One is an all-orange striped boy, and we named him Tito. The other is a girl, mostly black with white socks, and white on her face and chest. Of course, her name is Greta. When Luca and I sit on the sofa, Tito likes to sit on my lap and purr. Greta likes to drape herself on Luca's shoulders and purr. Needless to say, we're spoiling them.

Please stay in touch. Tell Cat that she and I can Skype occasionally and talk that way. And please come for a visit!

Lots of love,

Fiona

"That's so sweet," Cat said.

Miles nodded. "Yes. I'm very glad they are happy together." He sipped his coffee and smiled at her. "What about you? What are you doing this morning?"

"I'm looking at seed catalogs. I want to start a spring garden. How about you?"

"I'm writing my friend Gracie in Cape Town, South Africa. She sent me a copy of her new book, and she included an old-fashioned, handwritten letter. I'm going to return the favor. I'll send her a copy of my new book when it's available."

"Okay. I'm going back to my seed catalogs." Cat returned with the dogs to the kitchen, and Miles returned to the letter he was writing.

Hi Gracie,

So great to hear from you. Thanks so much for the copy of your new book. I'm really pleased to receive it and to receive your letter that was enclosed. I'll definitely read your book.

My first book will be officially published in the spring. I'll be sure to send you a copy. I'm already working on a second book. And, as I mentioned, I'm teaching, too, and my department chair put me on a couple of committees. So I stay busy. But learning to cook is a priority for me. I'm taking cooking lessons from Señora Consuela Romero. I'm thinking about writing a cookbook with brief cultural and historical information included.

Congratulations on your upcoming wedding. Your intended is a handsome bloke. His name is Jacob? So he's a university professor in history? What's his area of study? And he's from the Xhosa ethnicity? I looked it up. I read that Xhosa sounds like "ko-suh." Interesting. I'm happy for you. I wish you a long and peaceful life together.

As for me, I'm madly in love with a lovely Mexican-American girl here. Catalina Amalia Miranda. She's bilingual and bicultural and funny and sweet and sexy as hell. I'm trying to work up the courage to ask her to marry me. I want to be romantic when I propose, but I'm kind of hopeless in that department. I'm too much of an academic book nerd, so I don't really know how to be romantic. I'm almost certain that she'll agree, but I still want to make the proposal a really memorable event for her.

There's something serious I want to ask you about. I notice you are not teaching at a university. Is that because jobs are hard to come by, or did you intentionally decide to go in a different direction? I'm asking because I'm thinking of making a big change. I feel like I've been on a treadmill for years now. I knew early on that I wanted to study history and write books about history. That led me to university, then a PhD program, then a job teaching in a university with the expectation that I'd teach and write books so I could get tenure and keep my job.

But my life this past year or so has been so different from what I expected, and so rich and wonderful, too, that I'm thinking about getting off the treadmill. I'm thinking of quitting my job. I know that's shocking to think that an assistant professor at a respected university would just up and quit and go to live in a little town on the border with the woman he loves. Then I'll do what I really love which is to research and write books, and to cook. I'm seriously considering this major change in my life. What do you think? Am I totally stupid? Or am I a spirit on the verge of liberation?

You asked about Sonoran cuisine. Sonora is the northern-most state in Mexico, just across the border from the U.S. state of Arizona. I'm just going to write about a couple of dishes rather than give you an actual recipe. I'll send a proper recipe later for this soup and also for some other dishes. Note that there's a lot of improvisation that goes on in the Sonoran cuisine kitchen. Every time I make a dish with Señora Romero, we seem to change it a little bit.

No doubt there are some items I know you won't be able to get in Cape Town. But there may be something to use as a substitute.

Let's start with the most important appetiser ever: guacamole. *There are many recipes for* guacamole. *In my opinion, all you need is garlic power (not garlic salt) and some sea salt. Peel the avocados, smash the interior pulp up, and add garlic powder and salt to taste. Eat with tortilla chips. Simple.*

Next is pico de gallo. *Pico de gallo translates as "beak of the rooster." I have no idea what that's about, but the dish is a culinary delight.* Pico de gallo *is a fresh sauce (*salsa fresca*), not cooked, made of everything raw: chopped onions, tomatoes,* jalapeño *peppers, cilantro, salt, and lime juice. Leaving the jalapeños out will make it less spicy but not as interesting. Add everything together and let it sit for a while so the flavors blend. You can eat it as is with tortilla chips, or add it to burritos, eggs, tacos, beans and rice, whatever.*

Moving on to sopa *(that's soup in English). Here's how you make chicken tortilla soup. First, soak and cook some black beans ahead of time so they'll be done before you start your chicken tortilla soup. Use leftover chicken, or precook chunks of chicken, or maybe use tinned chicken. Whatever you have. Shred the chicken.*

To make the soup, first sauté chopped onions, garlic, and jalapeño. Then add the chicken broth, tomatoes with their juice, the precooked black beans, the shredded chicken, corn (frozen or tinned), lime juice, black pepper, and salt. A lot of people also add chipotle *powder to the soup to add a little bite.* Chipotles *are roasted* jalapeño *peppers. I can send you some* chipotle *powder. Let the soup simmer for a while. Serve in bowls with chopped cilantro and cut up strips of tortillas added on top at the last minute. Variations: leave out the* jalapeño, *or add a chopped avocado, or add shredded cheese.*

Okay. That will get you started. Write me!
Your friend forever,
Miles

Thank you from the Author:

Hello Reader!

Thank you for reading *The Broken Pot*, the third Cat Miranda mystery. Please leave a review of this book wherever you buy books (Amazon, Kobo, Nook, Apple, etc.) and also at Bookbub and Goodreads. By leaving a review for others to read, you can make it much easier for mystery readers everywhere to find this book. Thank you so much. Please sign up for my monthly newsletter all about art, books, and the natural world at www.cjshane.com/contactnewsletter.html

About the Author:

C.J. Shane is a writer and visual artist based in Tucson, Arizona, U.S.A. She has worked as a newspaper journalist, an academic reference librarian, and an ESL teacher. She is the author of eight nonfiction books, and her fiction works include the Letty Valdez private investigator mystery series and the Cat Miranda cozy mystery series. She's working now on a new series called the Iron Horse Mysteries. See more of Shane's art at https://www.cjshane.com/art.html or at BajaArizona Treasures on Etsy.